MISE EN DEATH

a Bittersweet Mystery

NIKKI WOOLFOLK

MISE EN DEATH

A Bittersweet Mystery

Book One

By Nikki Woolfolk

BITTERSWEET MYSTERY SERIES

1881 – 1882 HONFLEUR, LOUISIANA

Each standalone novel follows the adventures of everyone's favorite Steampunk Chocolatier and amateur-sleuth Chef Alex LeBeau. This culinary mystery series is filled with risque humor and witty characters set against a diverse world.

WICKED NIGHT CARNIVAL
PRESENTS SERIES

1880 – 1883 INTERNATIONAL

When the circus comes to town, secret agent Eva Merchant
and her troupe are there to entertain while using their smarts
to thwart villainous plots to take over the world while leaving
friends and foes breathless

CHOCOLATE

To SHOP for Artisanal Chocolate, Candy, Chocolate Chai,
and more go to: BelleMondeChocolates.com

MISE EN DEATH. Copyright © 2017, 2021 by Nikki Woolfolk. All rights reserved. Printed in the United States of America.

www.NikkiWoolfolk.com

Designed by Bookfly

Library of Congress Cataloging-in-Publication Data
Name: Nikki Woolfolk, author
Title: Mise en Death / Nikki Woolfolk
Description: Trade Paperback | Connecticut : Word Nerd Press, 2017, 2021

Identifiers: ISBN: 9780692943519 (Trade paperback) | ISBN: 9780692943526 (e-book)
Subjects: Historical Fiction

Word Nerd Press books may be purchased for educational, promotional or promotional use. For more information please contact Info@NikkiWoolfolk.com

First Edition 2017
Second Edition 2021
10 9 8 7 6 5 4 3 2 1

For Menashe- For Upside Down dancing whenever I ask. Always.
For Nerd- Whose love is always leading me back, e.s.
For Brian- For being my rock that intense November in '11. I
miss you.

A NOTE FROM THE AUTHOR

Dear Reader,

Thank you.

Often author's notes are filled with a long message, and this one is no different. I figure it best for me to sum it all up with those two words in case you are eager to jump into reading the novel. If you are looking to read each page in order or skip back after you've finished the book please do continue to read on.

In my close circle of friends, it is no secret this novel is not only a labor of love but a story I fought to bring into your hands for quite some time. Almost ten years, but who's counting those days and nights? It is hard to write about the things you love when your life is filled with handling the chaos and real-life Shakespearean tragedies. That said, what kept me going was wanting to read a book that uplifted me through all of it. I wanted to read a book that made me laugh until I cried and inspired me to create art.

They say the first draft is for the Author and the final book is for the Reader. I agree. Dearest reader, I hope you enjoy the adventure and have made sure to eat before reading. My beta readers have often informed me that reading my stories can put a reader's diet in jeopardy. Consider yourself forewarned.

Literarily Yours,

Nikki Woolfolk

CHAPTER 1

**Honfleur, Louisiana
Summer Solstice eve, 1881**

If it had not been for the ice cream, Alex LeBeau would not have found herself in jail.

On the last leg of their journey from up north, Alex's young son, Pierre, drove them along the outer road of her childhood parish of Honfleur in their steam-powered automobile. The brass and steel bonnet of the contraption gleamed in the June morning sunlight and caught stares from the many town patrons enjoying their mid-afternoon constitutional.

In the passenger's seat, with a hand firmly grasped on her almond wafer cone, Alex used her free hand to adjust her goggle strap against the back of her humidity-dampened Eembuvi-style auburn plaits.

Despite the speed of the automobile, the breeze was stifling and caught at the back of her throat. Or was it a bug?

Grimacing at the thought, she licked at the frozen concoction. The sticky caramel and sea salt blended together in her mouth, and she let out a euphoric sigh then took another lick.

Pierre pulled the handkerchief from his breast pocket. "Here, you've dropped some ice cream on your skirt," he offered, slowing the car as he waited for a pedestrian to cross. "*Maman*," Pierre playfully chided as he adjusted his own goggles.

She gave a soft *merci* before taking his handkerchief and used it to swat at the two bees hovering at the hem of her skirts.

"*Bon Dieu!*" Alex hopped out of the mobile. Holding her ice cream in one hand, Alex fanned her skirts with the other. She did not notice the sound of the car stopping or the quick footsteps behind her. Her focus was on the angry bee up her skirts.

Alex gathered up a fist full of material and flung her hand upward with such force her fist connected with Pierre's jaw. He fell to the grass like a stone. Alex stopped and gasped at her unconscious son as the two bees flew from underneath her skirts. She glanced up to notice the two police officers staring at the scene with humorless eyes.

She dropped her skirts.

"*Merde.*"

Alex glanced at one of the police officer's belt, spying the hydraulic D cuffs; her hands still faced the cloudless sky. The other officer knelt down at Pierre and checked his pulse before giving her partner a side-eyed glance. "Alive but out cold. We should get him to the station. Once he wakes, we can find out what happened."

The officer standing only a few meters away glanced at Alex. "Mademoiselle, we need you to come with us."

. . .

Alex hitched up her skirts slightly to cross her legs as she sat at the foot of the cot without any worry. Hunter and Lan the Wire Witch made sure to keep any of her past hiccups with the law off the police records. Alex may have cut ties, but Bellicose Solanum always took care of their own and kept their promises.

She knew with certainty nothing of her past would be found.

The odd thing about clandestine groups like BelSol is that they brought attention to themselves in ways Alex had never expected. BelSol posed as a night carnival that traveled by train. It housed some of the cleverest minds in the country.

Alex convinced the police officers to let her son rest, but while Officer Potkiss took notes, Officer Meckelson still questioned her in the station.

Meckelson stood a few inches shorter than Alex, but the height difference was lost as the officer sat on the corner of the desk.

"What brings you to Honfleur with an automobile full of weapons, Mademoiselle...?"

"LeBeau. My knife case of my best cutlery is only a weapon to the finest selection of beef or pork," Alex said with a laugh.

The officer's gaze bore into her. "If I were to get on the horn with Monsieur Guillaume, do you think this story would match up?"

Alex raised an auburn-kissed eyebrow and looked up into Meckelson's unreadable face. "There's only one way to find out that I am assisting Chef Guillaume at the Honfleur Cooking School. The Head Event Chef Heston up and quit, but do not take my word for it." She stood. "I need to check on my son while you make your call."

The other officer, Potkiss, did not stop entering data into

the Babbage machine at her desk. In fact, neither Potkiss nor Meckelson pressed further in the query as Alex joined Pierre in the jail cell. Alex had enough run-ins with the police to know when they were trying to intimidate and shake up someone. Alex was no fool.

She peered out the small window, watching a lady in britches riding a velocipede in a circle around her friends, laughing and teasing them as she feigned loss of control of the dual-wheeled contraption.

Alex peeked at the chronometer on her wrist. Even if Pierre woke soon, she would be late getting settled at her mother's before preparing for tomorrow's event.

It could be worse, Alex thought.

Though Alex was fully aware her privilege could not protect her son *per se*, she could use it for something good.

As a Creole woman in this post-Insurrection, she was aware of her privilege over Anglo men and their ancestors who created the causes for the uprising in the first place. Oppression, slavery, or any forms of inequality against Black, Brown, and Indigenous folks ceased after the Insurrection of 1856.

Any Anglo men with a desire to create or fix anything more than a calculating machine required heavy licensing fees. Even if any Anglo male had the rare fortune to have a few coins in his pocket, the mounds of paperwork and psychological evaluations would break his spirit.

Attempted genocide of the Native peoples and the dehumanization and enslavement of people from the Motherland drove the policies and regulations of the new America.

"Ma'am," Officer Meckelson said.

Alex faced the hard-jawed brunette.

"Is there a reason you are carrying this many knives?"

"What kind of cook would I be if I did not have my own

knives? I cannot chew my way through animal proteins with my teeth."

The officer's eyes had lost their coldness. Meckelson aimed a thumb behind. "But Officer Potkiss can."

Alex blinked in surprise at the change in her mood and stifled a giggle.

Officer Meckelson unlatched one of the trunks and began to search through it.

"Please take care," Alex warned. "Those are gifts for my family."

Officer Potkiss peered over Meckelson's shoulder as they sifted through the decorative tin.

"Do I need to be warned about the contents of this tin?" asked Meckelson.

"Only if you are watching your sugars."

Both officers stared back at Alex.

"There's a six-piece pie collection. Apple, key lime, peach, blueberry, strawberry, and pecan ganaches covered in chocolate."

Meckelson pulled the clear, cylinder case out for closer inspection. Potkiss opened the top, looking at the two levels with six wedges, all colored with distinct pictures.

Each tri-shaped wedge was painted with either apples, strawberries, or limes and other cocoa butter silk-screened decorations.

Officer Potkiss searched through the tin and plucked out a couple of chocolate bars. One was labeled Apple Toffee and the other Tropical. The wrapping art on the bar showcased a coconut, the newly imported pineapples from Hawaii, and a tiny pinkish-red bumpy fruit.

"What's that?" Officer Potkiss asked, pointing to the fruit.

"Lychee. Looks odd, but its white flesh inside is so perfectly sweet."

Meckelson pulled out the five-piece box of chocolate and read the flavor map aloud.

"Saffron pear pâte de fruit."

"It's pronounced 'fwee,' not fruit."

"What is it?"

"Pureed fruit boiled down into a concentrated flavor."

"I see," Meckelson replied and continued reading. "Kumquat with Scottish shortbread cookie."

Potkiss leaned in. "What's this one with the yellow flowers and bumblebee pattern on this square one?"

"Oh, that's just my version of Honeycomb candy. A British treat with an American twist. The white flower with the green background, that's one I call 'Sakura Plum.' That is cherry blossom and plum tea marshmallow. And that last one, with the fleur de lis, is a traditional bittersweet chocolate with a buttercream ganache that melts just so in your mouth."

Potkiss looked at the chocolates then at Alex. "You make these?"

Alex flashed a smile. "Yes. Those are a test batch. I would like to have my own shop one day."

Meckelson and Potkiss' eyes lit up.

The stationary voice telegraph rang.

Both officers did not move.

"Can someone answer that?" an officer called out from a corner desk.

Out of the corner of her eye, she saw Pierre stir, most likely from the bell chime.

Pierre rushed to sit up. Dazed, he took in his surroundings and finally rested his gaze on his mother.

Alex looked at him and shrugged. "Desolé."

He grimaced.

"It's Miss Miel, the madam of the Wild Mare brothel. She says Miss Clackett keeps telling her she has permission from her mother to be at the brothel farm down the ways."

The second officer turned from Alex. "What in the world? Isn't her mother in her late nineties?"

"Why don't you ask her when we get there?"

"Miss Clackett brought her own mother to a brothel?"

"Yes, and several more of her friends from the retirement home. Miss Miel says they're making a scene because they only have enough money for one gent to rent, and there are eight ladies."

Officer Meckelson turned to Alex. "You two will be all right. Keep ice on that jaw of yours, son, and next time, stay out of the way with your *maman*. She's got one hell of a right hook."

The officers exited out the front entrance as Guillaume was stepping in. All three did a roundabout in the doorway before exiting or entering.

"Ellec! It's so wonderful to see you again. What did I miss?"

Pierre looked at his mother, and Alex avoided his gaze to embrace her friend.

With Guillaume's accent, he had pronounced her name as Ellec for as long as she could remember, and it never occurred to her to correct him.

"I will drop you off at Maman Eloisa before taking you to *l'ecole*, all right?" Guillaume said.

"I'd need to get started on the menu."

"Your *maman* would have my head if I did not let her see her daughter the moment she got back into town. We go, you drop off your things, then come to the school," Guillaume said.

Pierre took the time to enjoy being a passenger in the front seat as Alex sat in the back with her legs curled underneath her pistachio green skirts like a lounging cat.

The welcomed scent of the sea grew stronger as the drive progressed. Where New Orleans had shotgun homes,

Honfleur was surrounded by homes of numerous sizes on stilts to anticipate high tides and the occasional fifty-year flood, or worse, the yearly hurricane.

The clouds parted, allowing the sun to beat directly onto her uncovered head and burn her eyes. She reached for her leather-strapped goggles, still sitting atop her hair, and pulled them over her eyes.

Wearing a hat in a convertible was the practical thing to do, but for Alex, such things proved disastrous. After losing too many custom-made hats on the initial test drive out, she had given up wearing them. Grateful for her tinted goggles, Alex took in the sights of her hometown.

Half a dozen years had come with changes, and Alex took note of the new buildings arising or old eyesores missing from the landscape.

Guillaume slowly drove into the U-shaped pathway and stopped the car parallel to Maman Eloisa's front entrance. Pierre stepped out first, offered his hand to his mother as she unwound herself from the backseat.

"Boy, lemme look at you," Maman Eloisa called from the porch.

Alex glanced up at her mother's pride-filled face.

"Granmère!"

Pierre dropped his own mother's hand, leaving her in a lurch, before running to the matriarch of the family.

Alex rolled her eyes and closed the car door. Guillaume winked at Alex before removing their bags from the boot.

Alex allowed Pierre and Maman Eloisa to say their hellos, but the minute they were done, she barreled into her mother and hugged her tight.

At five feet ten inches, Alex towered over her mother, who was barely five feet five inches.

Pursed lips on an ageless brown face stared back at Alex

when she pulled away. Steely dark eyes stared back into Alex's hazel eyes.

Alex draped her arms around the older woman's neck.

The hard line of her mother's mouth softened.

"My girl, if I had stayed quiet for another minute, you would have spilled all your secrets, yes?" Maman said then chucked Alex softly under the chin.

Alex pouted as her mother returned the embrace.

"That wasn't funny," Alex said.

Maman pulled away and looked Alex in the eyes, as if challenging her to remain upset. Alex immediately acquiesced and gave her a smile.

When Alex had been Pierre's age, she could not wait to explore the world, travel, and come back to tell Maman Eloisa of her adventures. In Alex's once youthful view, Honfleur had seemed too stagnant in people and outcome.

Though when she had been faced with unexpected parenthood amidst her travels, she found her desire for changing scenery waning.

Alex let out a sigh, and her mother did not protest being squeezed.

"Let's get inside," Maman Eloisa said and guided Alex and Pierre up the steps and into the house.

All four people stood in the tiny entryway of the house, but only Maman Eloisa did not look too robust for the space.

"Maman, we have got to get to the school. We have—"

"To eat," her mother finished. "You need to eat."

The males filed out of the foyer and towards the kitchen in an attempt to not catch Maman Eloisa's ire.

"Maman, I am fine."

Dark eyes stared back at her then looked at Pierre. "Pierre, dear?"

Pierre popped his head out sideways from the pantry door. "Granmère?"

"Did your maman feed you this morning before you arrived?"

Alex closed her eyes. He would sing like a canary and have no remorse.

"Oh yes. We, no, I had two different eggs, some grits, a couple of sausages, some bacon that was crispy at the hotel we were staying at, but the eggs were runny. Too runny, not like yours, and they burnt the seven sausages they had left. I asked them for more but they said that was all they had left so I ate them. Though I am still hungry."

"And what did your mother have to eat?" Maman Eloisa sweetly asked him.

"She had..." he stopped, thinking. "She had a piece of bacon and the ice cream from this morning," he supplied before going back to rummage through the pantry.

Maman Eloisa slowly turned her head towards Alex and crossed her arms. Despite wearing a full skirt, Alex could see the shift of fabric as her mother put out a hip. "Goodness, I am surprised your mother did not pop from such a hearty breakfast."

And there it was.

Alex's lips were a thin line. It was best not to open her mouth and experience her mother's food guilt monologue.

Maman Eloise walked to the kitchen.

"Mister Guillaume, how would you like your eggs?" Maman Eloisa asked.

Guillaume's eyes lit up. Alex could guess he had already eaten breakfast that morning before coming to see her at the station, but what was a chef who did not enjoy food?

"Maman Eloisa, anything you make is just perfect," he exclaimed. "Do you have those little sausage patties I like?" he asked, following her deep into the kitchen.

"Alex, get those trunks upstairs, and then grab an apron and help us in the kitchen," Maman Eloisa instructed. Her gaze never left Guillaume as she placed a hand on his while nodding an affirmative to all his food inquiries.

Alex was the award-winning chef, but her mother was a cook and a damn fine one.

Alex trudged outside and began the daunting task of carrying filled trunks up the nine steps while in skirts. After her third slow pass, those nine steps felt infinite. They had only planned to stay for a few weeks until Guillaume found a permanent replacement instructor for the Autumn semester.

Why had her son packed as if the visit was forever?

With the task complete, Alex took a kerchief from a hidden pocket in her skirts and wiped her dampened brow. A nice, cool bath would have been a good finish to the labor of settling in, but such a leisurely action would not be welcomed.

Her stomach growled at the idea of missing Maman Eloisa's cakes and perfectly cooked sausages. Alex surrendered to the call of a home-cooked meal by walking back into the house, grabbing her apron, and pulling the dishes out of the cabinet to set the table.

An hour later, plates of food, plenty enough to feed a dozen people, filled the center of the dining room table, not the four people seated.

"Hand that to your momma," Maman Eloisa said to Pierre as she passed a fixed plate into his hands.

"Maman, I am not that hungry. I—"

The deep lines around Maman Eloisa's mouth twitched, her face void of expression as she looked her daughter in the eyes.

Alex sighed, took the plate from Pierre, and began to eat. Despite the protest her mind put up, her stomach had missed the taste of home. It missed it so much Alex had a heaping second helping. She pretended not to see the smug look on her mother's face as she stabbed a sausage with her fork.

"Guillaume?"

He looked at Alex. "Oui, my dear," he said, fixing a third plate for himself.

Alex finished chewing before she spoke. "Have you seen what is on the menu tomorrow? What am I navigating the guests and students through?"

Guillaume took several bites, chewed, swallowed, took another few bites, chewed, and then swallowed again.

"Guillaume!"

Pierre and Maman Eloisa laughed behind their drink glasses as they feigned taking a sip.

"Oh, oh yes," Guillaume stuttered then wiped his mouth. "Chef York worked with Chef Heston on it."

Alex let Guillaume wax poetic for several minutes.

Guillaume stopped and looked at her. The lift in his eyes turned to concerned. "I do not like when your eyebrows do that thing."

Alex blinked. "What thing? My eyebrows do not do a *thing*."

"Yes. They. Do." Guillaume replied, emphasizing each word. "Your eyebrows do a thing whenever you do not like a menu."

He made a hand gesture to the space in between his own eyebrows and then made a motion toward her own.

"A month was spent on crafting this menu before you arrived, but in less than..." he glanced at his pocket watch, "less than eleven hours before the event, you want to change everything, yes?"

"Maybe," Alex said before taking a sip from her own drinking glass.

The water had already been consumed by Maman Eloisa and Pierre, yet their own glasses were still to their lips, their wide eyes following the exchange.

Guillaume softly cursed in French under his breath then abruptly stopped. "My apologies, Maman Eloisa."

Maman Eloisa did not look nonplussed. In fact, she shrugged her shoulders as if to indicate her daughter had that effect on people and to just accept it.

"The menu is perfect," Alex said.

"Yes. Yes, it is. So what is the problem?" Guillaume half shouted.

"That menu is meant for enjoying on the ground, not in the air."

Guillaume's face began to grow red as he waved his short, stubby hands around in exasperation. "What, what is this you mean, on the ground? On the ground, in the air. It's food, it's on the menu, the food—"

"Will be bland when guests eat it."

Guillaume blinked, his hands stopped waving. "What?"

Maman Eloisa and Pierre put down their empty glasses.

"The food will be bland," Alex repeated. "It's the altitude that will cause this reaction. You ever hear of xerotomia?"

"When flying," Alex continued, "one loses about a third of their taste. We would have to add a large amount of salt for guests to taste them."

Guillaume's eyes widened in horror. "Salt? Salt!"

"Yes, and the guests would be more bloated than the airship they're on."

Guillaume looked ready to swoon. "Perhaps we should use strong flavors and spices in order to compensate."

"Would you be opposed to offering a Middle Eastern cuisine to the guests?"

"At the school, we can get the clay oven fire stoked and make either Tandoor or roti. I will speak to Josephine about stoking the clay oven. Roti and desserts will complement the entrees, yes?"

Both smiled dumbly at each other, giddy in the throes of creating a new menu.

"You should probably let Chef York know before he and those students get their feelings hurt finding out about the change," Maman Eloisa offered.

Guillaume nodded. "Let me handle it."

"At least it is the day before the event," Alex said, helping to clear the dishes. "That gives us enough time to take the produce and proteins we do have and change the recipes."

"Not we, you," Guillaume said, eating the last piece of bacon on the plate before Alex took it away. "Oh, I remembered to bring the papers so you can look at the notes and test scores from your student's recent practicum. Then on Monday, you may help them brush up on skills and guide them how you see fit. I trust your judgment."

Guillaume rose from the table.

"Once I change into something fresh, you and I will go to the school. I want to see how much I can prep and finally see the cookery," Alex called from the dining room to Guillaume.

Guillaume came back in with an accordion file.

"Place it at the head of the steps, and I will get to it."

In the kitchen, Maman Eloisa stood and started to fill the sink tub with water to wash the dishes. Alex pushed Pierre towards her mother.

"Pierre will take care of that," Alex said.

Pierre turned and looked at Alex in disbelief, but Alex widened her eyes in mock innocence and shrugged her shoulders.

"Maman?"

"Yes," Eloisa answered, handing a plate to Alex to rinse.

"Could you watch Pierre while I'm at the cookery today? I will take him tomorrow night so he can work with me in the kitchen like old times."

Pierre grabbed the wet plate from his mother and dried it with his flour sack towel. "Maman, I am not a child."

Maman Eloisa stopped washing a plate. "Mister Pierre, are you too mature to spend time with an octogenarian?"

Pierre opened and closed his mouth.

Guillaume took the plate from the young man's hands and stacked it with the others in the cabinet.

Alex rinsed the last plate and kissed her mother on the cheek. "I will try to be home early tonight."

Alex kissed Pierre's red cheek before she walked out of the kitchen, grabbed the file at the head of the stairs, and trotted up to her old bedroom to change clothes.

CHAPTER 2

Less than a half hour later, Alex and Guillaume walked to the cooking school. As was tradition, Guillaume filled her in on the local town gossip.

They strolled past the Wild Mare just as Officer Meckelson and Potkiss were gently escorting the gaggle of older ladies out the front door of the brothel.

"But we have not finished making our selection yet," Misses Clackett cried.

"I want a receipt," one of the other ladies in the group said.

"Euphegenia, you cannot have a receipt. No services were rendered," Miss Clackett corrected.

Euphegenia made a face.

"Every week the same thing," Guillaume explained once they were out of earshot.

Alex made a wish for a similar experience if she were blessed to reach old age.

The sign for the *Honfleur Ecole de Cuisine*, the only cooking school in the entire state, sat near the edge of the road. The school itself sat back over a quarter of a mile from the main road.

Both walked on the loose-pebbled pathway towards the two-story mansion-turned-culinary-school with partial student housing. The acres of land had exclusive access to the dock. Guillaume had found this jewel decades prior but did not have the capital to purchase it until three years ago.

Inside the five different painted colored glory of the mansion, it housed two dozen rooms converted into individual classrooms.

"Teachers guide the students," he said. "You all are to be mentors to the students. If we continue to garner students, I may have an auditorium built near the back of the school to host chefs from other schools and across the pond."

Until recently, even after he had the funds to buy the property, he kept working as if he were a first-year cooking student.

At Guillaume's school, no teacher was tenured. His instructors taught but still worked in the field. He had hired chef instructors that he had met on his travels.

Alex clapped her hands together. "Oh Guillaume, it is beautiful!"

He smiled with pride.

"Look at what you did. You managed to turn this wedding-cake-styled house into a celebration."

"We just finished remodeling the back homes for the incoming students for the autumn semester," he told her as they approached the stairs. "There's an exact amount of rooms for the exact number of students for now."

Alex rubbed her friend's shoulders and squeezed him tight. Guillaume's changes removed the residue of a slave history best not praised in keeping the house in its original state.

She took one last glance at the first level wrap-around porch before following him inside.

"Your morning sessions will begin at nine and end at noon. The students will have their lunch here for obvious reasons and can use the equipment as long as they put everything back as they found it," Guillaume said.

Alex made a note of it.

"Practical lessons begin at one in the afternoon and conclude at five o'clock."

If Alex had decided to give up her daily constitutional, she would never want due to the slow elevator and the abundance of stairs available at every wing of the building. She was grateful for the small blessing of the demonstration kitchens being located on the first floor and not on the second.

The kitchens were designed to be mirrored versions of each other. The eastern side was for the pastry module, and to the west was the savory studies.

Guillaume gave her a quick tour of the school accompanied with hand flourishes and waves. Alex knew that whatever she missed, she would have a chance to explore on her own.

"This is where you will be teaching our second-year students."

She gave a nod of understanding as they walked past both second-floor classrooms on the eastern side of the building.

"As I stated before, you will be giving demonstrations in the first-floor kitchen on the left-hand side. If you need anything, do not hesitate to ask another instructor for help."

Alex made a semblance of a sound that she was listening as he continued.

"The elevator takes forever, and the students soon learn to just use the stairs. Also, during the week, we have recreation classes for the local townsfolk, and students' internships consist of splitting their time at the student-run restaurant in the middle of town and providing cooked-from-scratch meals to those less fortunate beginning in the fall."

Alex turned and smiled at him. That was her Guillaume.

"No matter how many awards you get or how many stars your restaurant will receive, never forget that it is the people that make you better. Making food is full of life lessons, yes?"

"Yes," she agreed and hugged him. "I am so proud of you."

Guillaume patted her arm a few times in embarrassment over the praise.

"Go. Chef York is downstairs preparing with the students for tomorrow. I need to break the news to him before it gets too late."

Alex agreed and wandered off to discover the building and plan.

Quite aware of the difficulty of finding a qualified chef instructor for a school, Alex knew when a good friend is in trouble, you help. That's what one does for friends that are just like family. Even if it included catering a dinner party in an airship with no open-flamed stove or oven.

Challenges.

"...and he just never showed," Alex overheard a woman state in the classroom ahead of her.

"How rude," another voice, higher in pitch, replied.

Alex passed the wall decorated with different food etymology penciled and water colored.

"He had asked me to purchase the tickets. Said it was his favorite play and had the nerve to promise to pay me the night of the opening. Next time I see him, I will give him a piece of my mind. Not only did he stand me up but I am several dollars short because I could not sell his ticket minutes before the show."

"Hush up. I think someone's coming."

Alex strolled by the door and was going to pretend she

did not hear the conversation but realized how stupid it would be to ignore potential colleagues.

"Good afternoon." Alex walked inside the classroom. "I am looking for any leftover lesson plans Heston may have left."

Both chefs looked at one another then back at Alex.

"Where are my manners? I'm Chef LeBeau. I am taking over his position."

The first chef shook Alex's hand before finding her words. "Chef Cordelia."

"Chef Rose," the second chef replied.

"T-taking over?" Chef Rose asked but did not wait for a response to the first question. "So Chef Heston is gone? Did he say where to send his things?"

"I'm afraid your guess is as good as mine. Guillaume told me that Chef Heston just vanished. No note. No telegram. No anything."

The two were silent.

Alex searched the room, mentally attempting to think of something to say.

"How rude," Alex said.

Both chefs nodded in agreement.

"Oh, look at the time. I think the lesson plans can wait. I need to get things ready for tomorrow's event. I hope we can talk soon," Alex said, leaving them to vent.

Alex caught herself from stumbling down the stairs to retreat to her haven—the kitchen.

It was a Friday afternoon, and Guillaume did say that there were no on-site evening classes, so she had free reign of the area.

Finally downstairs, Alex slid the pocket doors to the student kitchen open. With her notebook under her arm, she grabbed a stool at one of the long worktables and sat down. After pulling her reading spectacles out of her side-arm pocket, she flipped through the binder to look at the notes she made along the side margins. The pastry and the bread flavor combinations were appropriate choices for sea level.

She studied the pantry and cold storage list. Checking for ingredients before crafting the menu was imperative. To keep peace with Chef York, Alex decided to add cold appetizers and a soup to the new menu. Items that could be made the day before without losing their flavor were always welcome.

With the first draft of the new menu written out for Chef York and Guillaume to approve, Alex decided it best to make a hostess gift for tomorrow's event on the airship.

When having to give unwelcome news, the gift of chocolate always softened the blow.

During their earlier walk to the school, Guillaume had told Alex, "Madam Brookmeyer could have hired a professional cook, but she chose us, Ellec."

"She is a big proponent of supporting science in local settings. She told me that the more attention she gave to locals and their businesses, the better chance they had of succeeding."

Alex had only heard of Brookmeyer in passing but believed Guillaume's words that she was 'good people.'

Good people deserved chocolate.

Despite the humidity in the air, Alex could make a quick batch of Port-infused ganache for hand-rolled truffles. She could set them up in the freezing unit if she could find it.

But first, chocolate.

It would need to be something deep and bitter to offset the sweet port wine. Perhaps a seventy or sixty-five percent Criollo and Trinitario chocolate blend from Venezuela, she thought. Guillaume always kept good couverture on hand.

The setup of the pantry was a standard walk-in, dry goods to the farthest corner and the refrigeration unit on its left.

She opened the insulated door and walked in, welcoming

the cooler temperature on her hot skin. The door automatically closed behind her. Alex checked to make sure she was not locked in before proceeding to gather a few supply items for her thank you gift for Madam Brookmeyer.

There were only a few hours to spare before she needed to be fully focused on everyone else non-stop for the evening.

Alex grabbed her items and pressed the door to open, but it didn't budge. Her heart thumped hard against her chest as she pressed against the unmoving door. Taking a deep breath, she leaned her shoulder down and with all her weight gave a quick ram towards the door. It opened before she made contact, and she slid across the tiled floor.

Fruit flew in front of her. Her hands were splayed out as she landed on her stomach with a thud. Her breath escaped her in an audible puff.

Coming to a full stop, she laughed and turned to face strong, muscular legs the color of dark hickory adorned with overly long socks with little plaid tags on the outer side of each leg. Blinking, Alex let her gaze follow up the sock owner's bare knees and to the blue and green plaid skirt and pressed, fancy white shirt. Her eyes rested on full lips stretched in a smirk.

Humor-filled eyes gazed at her.

"I prefer to pick my berries from the vine, not have them tossed at me," a soft accent said from above her head.

Alex blinked and looked at the small, leather-clad shoes standing a few feet from her. She blinked and tried to right herself. Long, brown fingers reached out to help her up.

With hesitation, she took the offered hand and stood. Alex's face was mere inches away from a woman whose skin was as dark as chocolate liquor.

"Are you all right?" the woman asked. "You took quite a tumble."

Alex watched the woman's lips as the words had an accent Alex could not place or understand.

"Pardon?"

The woman reached a hand out towards Alex's forehead. "Hurt? Are you hurt?" she asked.

"N-No," Alex stuttered when she felt the stranger's elegant fingers touch her skin.

"I think something was in the doorway. Oh, my fruit."

Alex ignored the stranger's inspection and gathered up all the fruit and put what she could into their respective baskets.

"Your fruit? You are working with Chef Heston?"

"Chef Heston quit. I'm replacing him. My name's Alex. Alex LeBeau," she offered, standing upright.

The slim woman took Alex's free hand. "Josephine Campbell."

Alex looked down at the very short dress Josephine was wearing. "Do you always wear a dress when opening the walk-in refrigeration unit?"

Josephine chuckled. "It's not a dress; it's a kilt."

Alex knitted her brow. "I don't know what you just said. Are you speaking English?"

Josephine chuckled. The ball on top of her wool bonnet shook. "Madam, I was thinking the same of you."

"Alex."

"Pardon?"

"Not madam. Just Alex."

Josephine nodded. "Right. Alex."

The way her name sounded on Josephine's accented tongue made Alex want to surrender to anything ever asked of her whether clothed or disrobed.

"Where am I putting these?" she asked, pulling Alex out of her thoughts.

"Wha- Oh...uh, on the draining board across from the stove. I just need to find the port wine. I stepped in for Chef

Heston for tomorrow evening's airship dinner. I thought it would be nice to give the hostess a thank you gift for having the school cater the event."

"I see."

"I don't need much."

"Pardon?"

"Port. I don't need much for the gift. It's only for her."

"Ah. Any specific kind or, wait, this is your first day. Do you mind if I pick it out?"

An oddly dressed woman in plaid who she didn't know from Eve was asking if Alex trusted her wine choice.

"Yes. Absolutely. Are you going to a costume party?" Alex asked.

Josephine furrowed her eyebrows then lifted them. "Oh, no," she said with a laugh.

Alex flushed. She just insulted her.

"This," Josephine gestured to her body and ensemble. "It's my family's proper dress attire for special occasions. I've got mah kilt with the Campbell colors. Mah sporran and my tam," she finished.

As if to drive home the point, Josephine shook her head to make the little ball on top of her bonnet jiggle.

Alex's cheeks flushed in embarrassment for not knowing. "What is the occasion?"

"Summer Solstice celebrated the Scottish way. You know, bonfires, lots of food, drink, and an uneven number of bagpipes played at random times."

She laughed. She had no clue what a bagpipe was but liked how Josephine's voice rose and fell and was filled with mirth. "Aren't you hot?"

"Oh, gods, yes!" Josephine replied. "But you get used to it. I just came in to pick up a few things before stepping out. It's going to be a long night today, so I needed to make sure things were taken care of because I will not be in until late tomorrow."

"You're a fellow chef?" Alex asked, her voice unable to contain her hope. Visions of a kilted chef sprang into Alex's mind.

Josephine chuckled. "Oh no. For the life of me, I canna cook like you lot, but I can garden."

That would explain Josephine's grip.

"You are the potager," Alex happily surmised. "You make stock and maintain all those gardens in the front? You are quite skilled. I did not get a chance yet to see the different herbs you have planted."

"Perhaps when you have the time, I can show you around the garden. My pumpkins are growing quite fine if I do say so myself."

"I would be happy to look at your pumpkins." After the words left her lips, Alex realized that the comment could be taken in a lewd manner. She decided not to entertain the thought or go down that train of thinking. *Besides,* she told herself, *Josephine started it.*

"You're the Josephine Guillaume told me would stoke the fire," Alex blurted out.

"Come again?"

Alex shook her head. "Guillaume told me he would ask Josephine to stoke a fire in the oven to get the bread made for the roti."

Josephine lifted her chin. "Aye. I can stoke a fire."

Alex blinked at Josephine and pressed her lips together to keep from saying something inappropriate.

"Is there anything else I can do for you, Miss LeBeau, before I go?"

Stay.

"Alex, and no. Thank you for your help."

"I would invite you to the celebration, but it looks like

you have your hands full tonight with the event. I'll work on the fire before I leave."

Alex nodded apologetically. "Yes."

"Nothing like being thrown into the lion's den on your first day," Josephine said.

Alex nodded in agreement. "As challenging as it may be, I must admit it cannot ever be the gingerbread fiasco I witnessed last Christmas."

Josephine raised her eyebrows.

"In all my years, I have never seen that many tears coming from so many grown men. A cacophony of frustration all in one room was almost too much to bear," she said.

Then added, "Food is supposed to be about having fun. If I learned anything that day, it was to bring extra handkerchiefs and never believe any local townsfolk when they ask you to judge a friendly gingerbread house making competition."

Josephine attempted to suppress her look of bemusement. "I'll keep that advice in mind."

Alex smiled back.

"The fact that you got out alive is something to be grateful of, yes?"

"Absolutely."

A silence fell over them, and neither woman felt the need to interrupt its comfortableness.

Alex looked into Josephine's umber-colored eyes. She seemed to be on the verge of asking something, and Alex held her breath. Waiting.

Then the silence shifted, and a coldness fell behind Josephine's gaze.

"Well," the Scot said. "I must be off. A pleasure to meet you, Chef Alex."

"Alex," Alex squeaked out.

The minute Josephine left the kitchen, Alex berated herself for acting like a schoolgirl and fawning over a strangely dressed and oddly accented beauty of a woman. After the last batch of romantic trouble years ago, Alex had sworn off courting.

Alex promised herself to not be distracted by the first woman to cause her stomach to flutter like the leaves on a blossoming apple tree in a Spring breeze.

She needed to do what was in her best interests, and that did not involve chasing after a deceptively strong, fancy dressed warrior woman.

An hour later, as the port wine chocolate truffles chilled, Alex sought Guillaume out.

In the small office, Alex watched Guillaume study the menu.

At the head of all the decisions was Guillaume, who oversaw every business transaction for both the school and restaurant.

"My dear, you have outdone yourself. I see you are pulling from your time in Jordan with the soup. Chef York will not be able to say no," he said triumphantly.

Alex smiled back at him.

"I will give this to York in a moment, but you and me, let us make arrangements to get a sense of the airship kitchen. Madam Brookmeyer mentioned needing to be there early to set up some gift she purchased in Asia. I will go with you and make the introductions. Be ready mid-afternoon tomorrow. D'accord?"

"D'accord," she replied.

"Now, get some rest."

With sunlight still out, Alex took the opportunity to prepare dough for croissants the day after the airship event as a nice reward for herself and Pierre.

That evening in bed, Alex turned on the extendable light,

rotated its scissor arm, and got to know her students on paper better.

There were four that stood out to Chef Heston in terms of skill, which Alex had surmised due to three of the four being the names of some of the kitchen staff. Davian, Baxton, Mr. Jones, and Ren. Though when she looked at the list of students that would be on the airship, Ren was not on it. She'd have to ask about it later.

For the upcoming week, she needed to correct what they struggled with. Alex noted that Ren had an issue with presentation.

'*All dishes are completed in a timely manner though Ren would do well to learn how to work the plate,*' was all that Heston wrote for her.

The other notes were not as tactful for the three men. The word *snail* was written besides Mr. Jones' skill assessment, *boring* besides Baxton's, and Davian's was a statement: *Cannot follow recipes but has good memory.*

Alex had never seen such an odd assessment of students before in all her days of teaching. Though something about them must have been stellar to be chosen to cook on the airship.

Alex's eyelids began to droop. She placed the papers on the nightstand before snuffing out the light and drifting off to sleep. Her dreams were filled with endless stairs and doors that lead nowhere.

The next day after a leisurely morning of making too many blueberry muffins and crepes, Maman Eloisa and Pierre agreed to save the rest for another day. Stuffed, they took a stroll on the isle's sandy coast.

Though not a fan of life near water, Alex took comfort in walking alongside her mother.

How had she forgotten this simple pastime?

Alex glanced at her chronometer and made a mention of having to leave both Maman Eloisa's and Pierre's company. Once they returned, Alex left Pierre directions on where to be for the airship event that evening. Alex walked to the school to pick up Madam Brookmeyer's gift before getting to the hangar.

"Pierre's name is on the list," Guillaume said to Alex as she walked to him. "He is going in my place. I hate flying."

Alex chuckled. "Then why did you say yes to catering this event on an airship?"

With a shrug of his shoulders, Guillaume replied, "I like to not be in debt."

"Fair."

Much to Guillaume's chagrin, Madam Brookmeyer was not on the airship. The gentleman secretary said she was indisposed due to an impromptu meeting. The airship crew allowed Alex and Guillaume on board to get supplies into the kitchen before the event.

Both were led through the etched, stained-glass doors. Alex held her breath walking through the long dining room table that easily accommodated twenty-four people. A huge table sat in the center with a large lump covered with a cloth on top of it. Besides it not being her business, her hands were too full and her time too short to peek underneath. Perhaps she would be allowed to see what was under the cover during the event.

CHAPTER 3

An hour before the guests were to arrive, philanthropist Madam Brookmeyer directed everyone from all stations into their final tasks for the party.

"Do make certain fresh flowers from my garden are in all the rooms. The flowers are not fully bloomed, so add a penny to the water in each vase to assist," she instructed one of the airship wait staff.

Madam Brookmeyer's linen royal blue evening coat matched the tablecloth, and her earrings replicated the gold utensils. Alex did not disregard Brookmeyer's matching skirt's decorative gold braiding three quarters down, which matched the painted gold braid edging on the navy colored plates.

"Madam Brookmeyer," Alex interjected; she turned. "About the menu." Brookmeyer noted Alex's perfectly crisp white chef's coat. "Monsieur Guillaume informed me that the menu was to reflect the local route of the airship and your surprise would serve as the dessert for the evening."

Brookmeyer gave her a look as if to ask, "And?"

"While we do focus on pleasing our clients, I noticed that

the menu created, its nuanced flavors will not be fully appreciated by the palette at a higher altitude."

As expected, disappointment crossed Madam Brookmeyer's face. "I had chosen that menu specifically for the guests," she began.

Alex smiled. Menu items always sounded more special when said with an accent. All ingredients for the new menu were in season, meant less headache for all cooking staff, and were on Mr. Guillaume's budget.

"Instead, here is what your guests will enjoy this evening," Alex began then translated the entire menu into French. Madam Brookmeyer's eyes widen with surprise.

"Madam? Would you like to provide your own wine? We have a sommelier that can make suggestions if you so need them before the dinner party."

"No need. I have a wonderful bottle I brought with me."

Alex gave a curt nod of acknowledgement.

Things could not have been better even if they tried.

The evening's dishes were a contrast of warm hues of almond, cinnamon, and salmon with striking accents of aubergine and coral-colored tomatoes plated on the dinnerware. The evening's cuisine colors were as diverse as Brookmeyer's outfit.

Alex thought about her standard chef's uniform, tiny braids pulled into a thick braid then knotted into a bun at the base of her head. Yet Brookmeyer had not even noticed how opposite they were, which was often not the case with hosts.

Often Alex would need to play human shield to the screeching demands from an entitled hostess at the kitchen staff, but she was relieved to be working for a worldly hostess. Alex would have to speak with Guillaume to find out how he met this color-coordinated philanthropist and see if the school could cater more events for her.

"This is a monumental occasion. This is our victory,"

Brookmeyer had said when Alex noted the tag attached to the neck with a modest scrawl, "Rousanne 1880."

Alex was no sommelier, but she had never heard of such a wine. She hoped it didn't taste of vinegar when one of the students, Davian, poured it for the guests during the main course. Alex glanced at the cork to check for the inscription on the cork inside the bottles to verify that the bottles were from legitimate chateaus.

Opened bottles from Brookmeyer's collection aired in the galley.

The striking scent of honey and pear lingered in her nasal cavity. Obvious this would be a good pairing with the meal, but the elevation would make the flowery wine too subtle for the guest's taste buds once they reached their highest elevation.

Perhaps she could convince the captain to compromise flying at a higher altitude for the sake of good wine and food.

Word was spreading about the school restaurant providing better, more top-notch fare than the most non-intern based restaurants. *Cuisine du Monde* was asked to cater a big event on an airship for Harp Brookmeyer the third. Brookmeyer had started out making money with the Committee's military aviation program.

When the Committee could end the wars, they gave Brookmeyer a generous sum of money for his blueprints and sought more technology elsewhere. After his unexpected death, Madam Brookmeyer took over his legacy.

The kitchen was tight and bustling but in a familiar, timed way where everyone knew what ingredient preparations were expected, and everyone chopped, diced, measured, or sifted in accordance to the course they oversaw that evening.

All ingredients for the new menu were in season, which meant less headache for all cooking staff, and was on Mr. Guillaume's budget.

Mise en place.

"I would like to introduce you to the chef who will be presenting the food for tonight's event. Élie Karsci, Chef LeBeau," Brookmeyer said with a flourish of her hand in Alex's direction.

"Mr. Karsci helped me through my grief when he brought his invention to my attention almost a year ago."

Élie gave a cool smile, eyes looking at the reporters and not at Madam Brookmeyer. In fact, Alex noted, neither of them looked at one another but stood several inches away as if to not be associated with the other.

Élie and Alex greeted one another, and once again, Brookmeyer spoke. "What has brought you out of your room, Élie?"

"There is rumor there will be turbulent winds coming later in the evening while we are on route to the Damask Warehouse. Rueben's concern lies in believing the contraption will not be able to hold during such a disturbance. In order to anticipate an issue, I need to secure the base to the display table."

"Have you spoken with the pilots about this?"

"No, madam," Élie said, pushing his spectacles up the bridge of his nose. "But if this rumor is true, I need to secure the display."

Alex watched the eye contact between them. The words were straightforward, but there was something overtly formal in their physical proximity. The distance between them seemed forced.

Élie stepped closer to Brookmeyer and whispered, "The blueprints are safe. Do not worry."

Brookmeyer nodded and straightened.

"Where is Mr. Ormont? Where is Rueben?" Brookmeyer queried.

"Madam, he has become ill again. Last night's festivities have caught up to him."

Brookmeyer glanced at the chronometer tethered to her wrist. Her well-groomed eyebrows lifted. "Will Rueben be well in time for our dinner?"

"I believe so; he just needs a treatment to get him through this evening's festivities."

Alex noted the silence between them that seemed to be secret code for something that she could not discern.

"Dearest Élie, you alone will not be able to lift or move the contraption without assistance, and the guests will be arriving in a short while. Is there anyone that can help you?"

"Madam, no one has a permit to work on such a piece," Élie answered.

"My son Pierre does, well, he has a Guardian, but she will not be available until tomorrow to oversee him," Alex said then immediately regretted her words.

"There is no time. We must have help right this moment," Brookmeyer said aloud as if speaking to herself.

Alex wished she could have taken back her words but swallowed her regret as Brookmeyer leaned in close to Alex. "Then it shall be our little secret that your boy helps us."

Alex did not make a sound.

"I promise you it will not take but a moment, I am sure. Élie will keep an eye on the boy," Brookmeyer said.

Alex gave a small nod.

Brookmeyer addressed both. "Then it has been settled. Élie, Pierre will help you, and I shall see to Rueben and then speak to the pilots to make sure they have a strategy if we come toe-to-toe with nature."

Alex parted for the kitchen to fetch her son while Brookmeyer turned towards the guest's sleeping quarters.

"I know your tech Guardian Miss Reid is not here yet," Alex said. "And I'm certain she would have my hide if she found out you were working with advanced technology without her present," she was telling Pierre as they walked towards the observation and dining deck.

The area was filled with lush, upholstered, honey-colored furniture, and oak walls displayed a generous fine art collection. This room was created for someone that wanted to live in the cabin on the airship. Not like the circus train she worked on in which every compartment was tinier than her body tucked into the fetal position.

Glancing in the direction of the overstuffed chaise lounge chairs with its expensive upholstery made Alex weary to sit for fear of staining it.

Pierre followed her to the display table. "Then I'll make sure never to get caught; besides, it's more engineering and mathematics than technology per se, but I won't tell Miss Reid if you do not."

"I'd rather you not be accused of anything against your permit; perhaps I should stay with you until this is completed?"

"If you wish," Pierre politely offered. "Though the rest of the students need you, and I rather not take you away from them. It is their first time in an airship."

Alex's stomach lurched. "Well then, just be as quick as you can."

"I shall be fine," Pierre offered. "I promise to only stay focused on the task. Besides, there is no way I can hack into anything. This is a mere weight and lever deal. I promise."

Alex hesitated a few moments, her mouth opened to speak, but Pierre had already turned his back and was listening to Élie's direction with rapt attention.

Madam Brookmeyer pulled the heavy cloth off and tossed it aside. A wait staff picked it up and took it out of the room.

"Chef LeBeau, can you call your students into the room in around ten minutes? I have a surprise for them," Madam Brookmeyer requested.

Fifteen minutes later, Alex stood with her students in the dining room. All facing the contraption, all the students were wide-eyed.

Their focus held on the contraption, all in silence.

Madam Brookmeyer stepped in front of them all, looked to Alex then to the students.

Madam Brookmeyer slapped her hands together and said, "A very intricate, extremely detailed machine that does nothing but simply entertain."

The students looked at each other.

The petite woman gave them a dazzling smile. "I am Miss Brookmeyer! Welcome to my airship." She gave a slight bow. "Would you all like to see Mr. Karsci and Rueben's contraption before you are stuck in that tiny kitchen?"

The students hovered around the playful and personable Madam Brookmeyer.

Brookmeyer began pointing out the miniature pleasure wheel, the glider, and a heating element would heat the large, iron kettle. The kettle was almost shaped like an airship, but it had a temperature gauge attached instead of a propeller system. From the kettle, a large tube went towards a mesh box.

"What does the kettle cook, Mademoiselle?" Alex asked.

Brookmeyer's dark eyes beamed. "Popcorn. It can hold three and a half to five pounds of popcorn."

"Non."

"Yes," Brookmeyer insisted. "To accommodate being on an airship since open flame is not allowed."

"Madam? Are you using vegetable oil to fuel the heat?" Pierre asked.

"A very good question. What Mr. Élie and Rueben did was make sure to run it on steam. That is why it is on this bolted down table. If you peek under the table cloth, you'll see that big tube that it is attached to connects it to the airship's engine."

"But how do you keep the popcorn from scorching if you are not using any, I assume, oil internally or externally?"

"The moisture content from the kernels ranges fifteen to twenty-five percent and is used to heat the inside."

Such a delicacy being prepared in Alex and the student's presence would be worth all the hard work cooking without fire had caused.

"During my travels to China, I saw some street vendors making popcorn. See, this contraption is what surrounds this," Brookmeyer tapped the kettle. "It's the main attraction. They call this a Popcorn Cannon. Is it not amazing?"

Alex looked at the students focused in on the words.

"The vendor would put the popcorn kernels inside, close the lid tight, turn on the kettle over a fire. Or in this case a heating element. Once the kettle reaches a certain temperature, the vendor would remove the cannon and put it half way in the mesh box like this," Brookmeyer said.

"We tested this earlier today. We used this kernel."

Brookmeyer held open her hand and the students gathered around to see the mauve-colored kernels in her palm.

"Though I love the blue kernels because their yield is much sweeter," Madam Brookmeyer added before picking up popcorn that had fallen through the mesh from the cannon and into a bowl and offered it to the students.

"Go ahead. Try some. Don't be shy. You, yes you, the tall drink of water," Brookmeyer said to Pierre. "You've got big enough hands to take several."

The students and Alex obliged.

"Did you know that there are six distinct types of corn kernels?" Brookmeyer said. "One of them is black and produces the whitest popcorn I've ever seen!"

Just like her students, Alex listened intently to Madam Brookmeyer go on about the varieties of popcorn, including rice and pearl. She even waxed poetic about how well one bloom melted in the mouth comparing the butterfly to the mushroom.

"The butterfly is delicate, but the mushroom has a heartier shape, and I've seen it used in caramel popcorn treats."

Everyone consumed the light treat when offered and forgot about the reason they were on the ship in the first place.

Alex was not the favorite in reminding them. Once the demonstration was over and Alex had sent the students into the kitchen to prepare for the event, Brookmeyer asked to speak to Alex in private.

"Tell me, chef. Why was it you that had noticed this error and not the other chef I spoke to?"

"My guess is that he had never flown anywhere before."

Brookmeyer eyed Alex. "A fellow world traveler like myself, I see."

"I follow the cuisines."

"Ah," Brookmeyer said. "Chef LeBeau, I would love to hear about your adventures."

Alex began to blush at Brookmeyer's growing attention. "Perhaps another time. I must attend to the kitchen crew. Do you need anything else?"

"Dessert wine. What type of wine would go with popcorn? Red or white?"

"White," Alex said without hesitation before passing the quartet and heading to the kitchen.

The string quartet checked their transmitter packs and the cords connecting them to their respective instruments. The violoncello player had been wearing slacks, but the last time Alex had seen a violoncellist, it had been during fire performance at an adult-themed circus.

In the deep red and golden-yellow-striped tent, the cellist had worn a short, wide skirt hitched above her thick thighs. Her legs spread wide enough to hold the bowed instrument and play the low notes that wound through Alex that spring evening somewhere near the Maidu village mountain area in California. Whilst fire performers performed to the audience, the music that had circled them all on that unforgettable and fateful night concluded with hearts and promises permanently broken.

This quartet, seated on the edge of their chairs, adjusted their stands before one of the violins began his count. The ensemble began their electro-harmonic piece, and each pluck of the string and bow sliding across the strings made no threat to Alex. There would be no haunting tune that reminded her of the deep-seated longing for the unattainable.

This quartet all wore black trousers and skirts at ankle-length, played refined chamber music respectable for dinner guests to mingle without their saudade shaken to the surface. This quartet's light sound set a different tone for the evening's gathering by showcasing everything but themselves.

This quartet were not her friends turned family from months ago.

Alex pulled herself back into the kitchen and from her thoughts. In the brigade, she left the sounds of the chamber music behind.

Some time after the velvet cloth was placed back on the machine, the guests finally boarded the dirigible.

Each new arrival was stunned into silence upon spotting the three-foot-plus-long machine on display parallel to the dining table.

A miniature pleasure wheel, its spindle arms etched with

scrolling flourishes by light radiation emission pistol, stood in the middle, facing towards the guests. Each observation car held tiny, stained-glass cars, which Alex and the students had been told each made a different note when a marble dropped into one.

Everyone clamored to the machine to fawn over it.

Why hadn't Alex noticed the miniature diorama picnic scene around the base of the wheel?

Boiled egg was not in any of the courses, but the faint smell of sulfur lingered in her nostrils.

Breathless, the young, ginger-haired fellow offered his hand to Madam Brookmeyer.

"Percival Jones from The Pelican national newspaper. It is a pleasure to meet you, Madam Brookmeyer. My belated condolences for your husband."

Madam Brookmeyer received his handshake and thanked him for his kindness.

"Percival, is it? I am not the belle of this ball tonight. Perhaps you would prefer to speak with Mr. Ormont and Mr. Karsci for your paper. They helped to bring our project to fruition based on my late husband's blueprints. While it was his dream to see it come to life, I am grateful for Mr. Ormont and Mr. Karsci's talents that will make this dream a reality and in turn help so many in need."

Percival continued. "Your late husband was not known for his altruism, so this soon-to-be revealed invention that will help the masses seems out of character, would you agree?"

Flash!

Out of the corner of her eye, Alex spotted the quiet, petite, mulatto-skinned gentleman's hands alongside the out-of-fashion daguerreotype camera on the tripod.

Madam Brookmeyer reached for a beverage being offered by the airship wait staff. A small smile played at the corner of her lips. She took a sip, her hands unwavering and her gaze just as steady as Percival fired question after question. Alex had the suspicion she was prepared for such an interrogation guised as an interview.

"What brought about the drastic change? Was it an implication of his impending death? If so, does this imply that Mister Brookmeyer knew he was not destined for this world much longer and this was his way of making peace?"

Flash!

Alex turned to see the engineers' faces. Mr. Ormont gave a broad smile of the high praise, but Mr. Karsci blinked rapidly, the sallow skin at his jaw set. She caught Mr. Ormont's gaze. He stepped closer to Mr. Karsci; his smile became compressed.

Reserve set behind his eyes, giving Alex the impression she violated his privacy without action on her part, and she was relieved when he turned his attention back to the philanthropist.

Percival gave a quick look to the engineers, nodded.

"Yes, but before I do, care to answer what made you choose to do it in such a parish as small as this one? Why you chose to have a party in a ship instead of on land in a large dining hall?"

Madam Brookmeyer placed her delicate fingers against the middle of her appliquéd-fabric-covered chest and let out a laugh. "Dear heaven. Which question do you want answered first?"

Most guests laughed, but Percival's expression did not change. Madam Brookmeyer did not seem to care.

"Chef?" Baxton called.

Alex turned her attention to her student.

Baxton.

Boring, Heston's notes had said.

"We cannot keep the whipped cream from falling in this humidity."

A slow smile spread across her lips. "Come. I'll show you a little trick my friend in New Virginia taught me."

Baxton followed Alex to the kitchen as the photographer from the local paper announced themselves to nearby guests.

A couple of feet behind her, Alex overheard an exchange happening at the table.

"Madam Brookmeyer, it all looks so delicious," a bright-eyed Filipino woman with robust stature said as they were seated at the dinner table.

"These are only the hors d'oeuvres, my dear," Madam Brookmeyer replied. "Chef LeBeau is responsible for tonight's menu. Someone please call for her. She describes the menu much better than I."

As a wait staff member ran off, Madam Brookmeyer placed her hand on top of the eager guest. "My dear, what is your name? What brings you here?"

The young woman's smile widened. "I am the lead writer for our cookery school's newspaper, Eat Your Words. Our school Honfleur Cookery is catering the meal tonight."

"And your name?"

"Raven Miller. I am in my senior year at Monsieur Guillaume's school."

Madam Brookmeyer patted her hand.

Alex turned backed to the chatter, her attention split between the kitchen and the dinner party.

"Ah, Chef. We were hoping you would give us a detailed description of what is on the menu tonight."

"Chef, may I ask you a few questions for Honfleur Cookery's paper?"

She turned to the questioning reporter and gave a curt nod. Alex would never be a salesperson, but she had a knack for talking up other people, and this evening would be no different.

"Chef LeBeau, tell us what you made on the menu."

Alex gave a polite smile. "The students at the Honfleur cooking School deserve all the praise for their multiple-course Mediterranean meal tonight."

The reporter looked taken aback. "That's a risky choice to make for tonight. Any reason behind the decision?"

"Xerostomia."

The reporter, photographer, and security team were silent. Now she had their attention even if there was confusion behind their gaze. She paused for effect.

Always a teacher.

"Xerostomia," she repeated. "Is also known as cotton mouth. Once the airship reaches over ten thousand feet, food begins to taste bland."

The reporter looked up from their notepad, eyes in genuine surprise. "Is that so?"

"Yes. In order to accommodate Madam Brookmeyer's guests, we put together a menu that is rich in colors but also in flavor. I must tell you that the students are some of the most skilled I've ever seen in all my teaching career."

She continued her praise for the students, the school, and their owner, her trusted friend and ally, Monsieur Guillaume, before taking her leave.

Back in the kitchen, Mister Jones was preparing the steam sternos and began removing the cold dishes from the woefully small vapor-compression refrigeration system.

Mister Jones, *snail*.

As elaborately decorated as the dining and hosting area was, no designer ever thought to design a galley thinner than the lowest setting on a mandoline slicer. Though compared to the train kitchen she was huddled in for several weeks during the previous winter, this was a generous space.

While Alex longed to see the machine in all its glory and perhaps replicate it using chocolate as a medium, she had a job to do. The former instructor leaving without anything besides a terse note of leave upset Guillaume but perturbed Alex. The reason was not because of the need to overhaul the menu hours before the event, but not one word of parting to the students occurred.

Being an instructor meant being an example to students, who often were having their first experiences in a professional kitchen. Her and her peers' job was to be professional and not serve as a warning of what not to do.

She stepped into the doorway to see both engineers with their backs to the piece they had created.

"Mr. Ormont? Mr. Karsci? The name's Sylvia DeWinter," the flaming red-headed woman said before handing the engineers her calling card. "May I get a picture of you both by the machine?"

Rueben Ormont's face lit up; Élie Karsci let him stand slightly in front as they positioned themselves at the tail end of the machine.

Ms. DeWinter threw the cover over her head.

"How long did it take you create and complete this mechanical contraption?" her slightly muffled voice asked.

Rueben straightened his shoulders and said proudly, "Four months from sketch to what you see on this table. I fashioned each of the pieces from mundane items I found and crafted them into what you see before you."

"You do a lot of tinkering when not working with Madam Brookmeyer and Mister Ormont, Mister Karsci?"

Rueben's eyes gazed at Élie as if looking for answer.

"Absolutely," Élie said. "He is beyond talented. I am just a note taker. It is Rueben who has all the engineering knowhow. I am not the brains of this invention as Rueben," Élie supplied. "I have a mind for the business side, and artistic types need people like me."

Alex suppressed the urge to scowl at him and hoped her nodding looked convincing.

"Stay still, gentlemen," Ms. DeWinter demanded.

Flash!

Ms. DeWinter pulled herself from the cover, went to the two men, and shook their hands before they took their leave to join the other guests as every guest was called to their assigned seat.

She glanced at the nixie clock. "Get everyone into the kitchen."

Alex stepped out to the hall attached to the dining area to gather the rest of the students.

"All right, everyone," she said once all of them were in the kitchen. "We only have a few minutes. How many of you have traveled on a dirigible?"

Everyone but Mister Jones and Davian raised their hands.

Davian. *Cannot follow recipes but has good memory.*

She gave a nod to get them to put their hands down.

"First make sure you have everything ready at your station. Second, for those new to travelling by air, you may find yourself feeling airsick. If you feel light-headed or sick to your stomach, let your classmate know, and rest. I do not want you contaminating the meals."

She omitted the details that their senior student in charge of the rotisseur was unable to cook the beef and the entre meittier was not able to stand upright to prepare the vegetables.

"Contaminate? How can we do that if we're feeling si—Oh. Never mind," Davian sheepishly said.

"Last, when you can, enjoy tonight. Soak it all in. You are cooking on an airship!"

As if on cue, the airship began the slow rise. The students

swiftly went to either of the port windows to gaze out as the weights were removed from the airship. The light of the rising moon glittered on the surrounding bayou as they left the ring of magnolias that wrapped around the entire base.

A few minutes later, the frenetic energy of the kitchen picked back up but was more focused, like a waltz. Several courses were effortlessly served in this manner.

Everyone was so focused they did not hear a small voice trying to shout out over the drone of the flying airship. Nor could anyone hear over the natural noises of the kitchen.

Alex placed a copper bowl in the refrigeration unit then grabbed her pocked bib apron before going on a search for her favorite whisk.

"Chef, the fottaush calls for pomegranate molasses in the dressing, but I don't think we have it."

Alex stilled in the doorway.

"Make nice with the waiter in charge of preparing the libations, and borrow a bit of grenadine to substitute for the pomegranate."

Baxton nodded and left the galley as the rest of the students hustled to prepare bowls of spicy Egyptian red lentil soup served with a lemon wedge to give a tanginess to the earthy dish.

Everyone was so focused on their task and putting their dishes out they struggled to hear one another over the drone of the flying airship. The initial nervousness left the students as they found their rhythm in the small space and surprised everyone in how the time for dessert snuck up on them all.

Alex failed to hear over the natural noises of the kitchen and engine noise and jumped at the tap on her back.

Brookmeyer leaned in towards Alex's ear. "Sorry to startle you. Did you want to see the contraption run? I know you did not have a chance to see it before."

Alex wiped her hands on her kitchen towel then followed Brookmeyer out to the dining area.

"Oh and please thank your son for helping me earlier," Brookmeyer whispered as they walked towards the observation deck. "I will keep his assistance under my hat, and his Guardian is to never know, which is too bad. Your boy is quite clever and should not be held back by Committee policy and technology regulations."

Without effort, Brookmeyer called her guests' attention over the drone of the airship's engines towards her seat at the head of the grand dining table.

The guests' attention followed Brookmeyer's gesture to see the velvet cloth being pulled off the contraption. The guests gasped as the machine's brass glinted in all its wondrous glory.

"My gift for you from one of the most talented engineers, Rueben Ormont. I saw the popcorn cannon on a street vendor's cart in China, and when I came home, I told Rueben about it. From my crude sketch, Rueben could not only recreate what I saw to the letter but also do so with such ingenuity and fun. It is my pleasure to present tonight's dessert: popcorn."

One of the wait staff started the contraption, and the small ball bearing slid and wound down the hollow tubes, metal rods, and into cups and levers.

Each part of the joints displayed a piece in a carnival scene. Then, following, the next ball bearing leading to the next scene until a heavy hook grabbed at the opening of the cannon, releasing the popcorn with a loud boom.

The reporters and photographer, like the students earlier, jumped at the sound then clapped. They looked at their hostess to find Brookmeyer in her chair, wide-eyed and a growing crimson stain growing at the center of her chest.

Alex crossed to Brookmeyer, cradled the back of her head.

Brookmeyer's mouth moved, and Alex inched herself closer to hear. Nothing audible came from Brookmeyer's lips. Alex looked at the dying woman in her arms.

Brookmeyer let out her last breath. Her sharp eyes stared beyond. Alex said a quick prayer under her breath.

Madam Brookmeyer was dead.

CHAPTER 4

The airship tilted violently, sending the guests stumbling, reaching out to brace themselves. The dirigible seemed to be without a pilot.

The music stands, chairs, and dinnerware hurtled to the side of the airship, clipping some guests before tumbling to the corner of the room. But Rueben's machine stayed unmovable.

Where was the engineer Élie Karsci?

Alex, the dinner guests, and quartet attempted to right themselves. The ship swayed, and Alex pushed herself towards the kitchen. She grabbed her whisk before turning towards the door leading out.

"Where are you going?" Mr. Ormont demanded.

"Bridge!" She headed to the kitchen entrance and towards the cockpit.

The airship dipped then began climb. Alex clasped the copper balloon whisk handle in her left hand and climbed up the metal ladder. She hooked her right arm to keep from falling into the airship skeleton below.

The roar of the engines echoed in the mass. She could not

hear the struggle but saw it though the glass—a dark-clad figure assaulting one of the pilots.

Alex squinted and spotted a frightened Élie on his knees facing a safe. His nimble fingers turned the combination, starting then stopping. The woman reporter that called herself DeWinter was also there, her bright red hair askew. White-blonde strands spilled from underneath her now obvious wig.

The red looked like flames at her crown, and the blonde resembled fine paintings of angels contemplating the suffering of man...a furious angel.

Furious Angel jammed a gun barrel into Élie's shoulder, and he started again. She could see his mouth wide, shouting, but Alex couldn't hear him. A large knapsack sat against Furious Angel's back.

Élie opened the safe and pulled out items hidden by the metal door. The door beam hid the hand-to-hand exchange between a frightened Élie and Furious Angel as she pulled him from his knees and pulled open the door. Élie ran out of the door and onto the bridge way.

Alex staggered to the control room as it pitched forward. Her strong, long fingers clawed at the ornate railing leading to the windowed room, and she braced her legs against the door jam.

A fist connected with Alex's jaw. She released her grip and fell onto her back. Her vision black then a white blur, her focus settled on the gun aimed at her face.

Alex forced herself to roll onto her stomach. Inches away, the shadow of one of Furious Angel's mud-crusted boots swooped down with force towards Alex's hand. She pulled away, feeling the impact and hearing a ringing over the loud drone of the airship. Alex reached out at DeWinter's ankle, stumbled briefly but caught her balance. The action angered Furious Angel more, and she came for Alex with a vengeance.

"I said, hold it right there!" Élie shouted at them both.

Alex and Furious Angel turned. Élie was standing, looking at them, eyes wide and hand shaking with Furious Angel's gun. Shaky hands and fear made a dangerous combination for someone holding a gun, especially inside of an airship.

With one fire of the gun, they could all go up in flames, or at least go down quickly with a leaky bag.

Alex could feel the shift in mood from DeWinter. She had never intended to use the gun. Alex looked at Élie and then to DeWinter. DeWinter reached into the back inner pant waist then brought both hands up in a surrender motion in front of her.

Finally, some reason, even if it was coming from the madwoman who put them all in this position.

Alex ran behind, watching Furious Angel run at Élie.

"No!"

With one hand, Furious Angel shoved Élie out of the way and continued towards the open hatch and into the sky with no parachute. The pressure pushed the shock of red wig off her head and showed her white-blonde shock of hair against the growing night sky.

Alex held herself within the open doorframe, the wind blowing on her face as she watched the Furious Angel sail like a bird into the growing dark, barely clearing the trees. Alex could barely make out the silhouette before lights engaged on her shoes and the knapsack parachute released.

No use trying to pinpoint the exact landing site, but Alex made note of the general area. Assuming Furious Angel escaped on foot, Alex would make a mention if asked but noted it was not her place to tell the police officers how to do their job.

Alex helped the stunned Élie up and guided him as quickly as she could to the dining room.

The airship was tilting, and no one was guiding the dirigible. "Watch him," Alex told Pierre before heading for the elevator crew.

Alex staggered to the control room as it pitched forward. She clawed at the ornate railing leading to the windowed room and braced her legs against the door jam.

Inside, she grabbed the wheel. The lights surrounding the nearby marsh were pin dots. Pin dots growing larger because the ship's back end tilted upright like a cat's behind.

The unconscious elevator crew chief, laid out on the new brocade carpet, rolled forward and stopped with a thud against the dash of the control panel. She hoped they weren't deceased, but she was a bit too focused on not dying to worry too long.

The elevator and rudder wheels were shut off. She found the gas board, checked the ballast board while keeping a death grip on the wheel. She took a hard swallow, realizing how labored her breathing had become and loud enough to be heard over the unmuffled airship engine.

Her single, thick braid flopped over her shoulder and against her face. She tossed her head back, and the braid flopped behind her and then promptly fell against her cheek, unchanging her hair situation.

She needed help. She looked around for a telegraph to the mechanics, hopefully still alive and stationed in the engine car.

Alex rotated the mechanical acoustic device towards her mouth. "Is anyone there?"

Nothing.

"Is anyone in the engine room?" she shouted.

Silence.

There were plenty of places in her travels she had almost died, but this was the most fanciful. Unfortunately, no one would be raving about the dinner party after this if they survived. She would focus on damage control to celebrate surviving this nightmare, but until then, she focused on getting the blasted ship level.

"I cannot do this alone," she said under her breath.

The device cackled.

"Some of us are in the engine room trying to save lives while you choose to drink on the job!"

Alex blinked and stared at the device. "I beg your pardon! I never—"

Cackling escaped the engine room device. They had no idea of the murder or escape that just happened.

"Ma'am, do you know how to fly this ship?"

"Once. I flew one once. The Malcontent."

"Ma'am, didn't that explode into millions of pieces?"

Alex shrugged her shoulders. "Only after I landed it and got everyone to safety."

"Say yer prayers, ladies. It looks like we're gonna meet our Makers tonight!"

How fitting...she would die surrounded by chaos and smart-ass remarks.

Alex pursed her lips and focused on steadying the ship, grateful they weren't so elevated she lost consciousness unlike the last time she was on an airship.

Her braid became a plumb line of sorts as the ship lowered its ass with the help of the ladies in the engine room. When her thick braid fell in between her shoulder blades, her breath was quiet. The drone of the engine was calming.

"Ma'am!"

Alex jumped at the sudden sound, appreciative her bladder was empty.

"How's our elevator crew, chief?"

She gave a quick look down at the body near her feet. Holding the wheel steady, Alex bent from the waist and let the tips of her fingers search for a pulse at the neck.

Slow and steady. Though from the way the captain had

rolled when the airship was vertical, she was certain the elevator crew chief would need a steep cup of willow bark tincture to ease the pain.

She stood up and spoke into the device.

"Your elevator crew chief is alive, but she's still unconscious. Unless you have a copilot, it looks like I'll have to land this thing."

Alex heard a faint, "Lord, Saints preserve and keep us."

She thought better to swallow her pride and keep her mouth shut. In all fairness, she could not make a retort. While sure she would land the airship without incident, she could not guarantee the exact location not be on a body of water. She wanted to tell them they'd live but would have to keep the "if the alligators don't get you first" part of the statement.

"We are bringing her back to Honfleur," Alex called into the device.

Silence.

"What is your status?" she asked. Gaining an assessment would help get them safely back.

Surviving the trip back was the least of her worries.

How she was to handle the dead hostess in the dining area and keep Guillaume's school out of the papers, she was not sure.

Landing an airship in the dark without having her bearings seemed much easier than facing the inevitable chaos once they were safely landed.

Alex's cheek throbbed only a bit, but previous experience told her that in less than twenty-four hours, there would be pain and a bruise to mark this encounter.

The airship began to gradually descend, and unlike her previous experience, the ship was tethered without incident or explosion.

CHAPTER 5

Alex went to her students. With long strides and a half-run, Alex backtracked to the main entertaining area of the ship. The chaos of the guests had ceased. Soft sniffles from occasional crying broke the silence and the dull drone of the airship engine.

Most of her students stood near the kitchen doorway, eyes wide and brows furrowed in confusion. They didn't know what to do.

"Attention!" she barked uncharacteristically. "Madam Brookmeyer is dead."

The kitchen staff did not move, but many asked, "How?"

"Shot to the chest," Alex answered plainly. "I do not know why. One minute, we were looking at the contraption, and the next minute, she was—" she stopped then went running to the main dining hall.

In her absence, no one had covered the body.

"Davian," Alex firmly called out. "Please remove the dinner table cloth from the dry sink and cover Madam Brookmeyer's body. If that is too much to ask, I will do so."

"No chef. I can do it."

Davian was gone.

Alex walked to the group of students.

"Pierre, I need you to get the guests to the other section of the dining area. Make sure no one, including yourselves, touches a thing in this room. When they get here, the police will need to go through this entire space."

Alex looked at the group. "Forewarning, this is going to take some time. We cannot leave until the officers give us permission. Mr. Jones, Baxton, turn off the steamers, take items out of the oven and off the stove, but do not pack anything away or throw anything away. Are we clear?"

Both nodded.

"You have your tasks. You may go."

Each student shuffled away, suddenly focused on the assignment given to them. In her opinion, any task was better than having them think about having witnessed a murder.

Pierre.

Looking around, Alex spotted her son comforting Rueben, handing him a delicate cup of sparkling water, the other hand on his shoulder. Rueben blinked up at Pierre and took the cup. Élie stood beside the two, looking at Brookmeyer's uncovered body, eyes dry, nary a tear, but eyes filled with disbelief.

Behind Alex, Davian placed a tablecloth over Brookmeyer's body. She went to her son's side and in silence gently squeezed his hand. He squeezed hers in return.

Alex made her way back to the dining area; her students stood in the doorway leading to the galley, all in various forms of growing shock.

The engine ceased, and silence filled the cabin.

"When the officers get in, I want you to answer their questions the best you can amount what you saw and heard tonight. Even if it seems trivial or of non-importance, tell them," Alex quietly said to the students.

Each student nodded numbly.

"Do any of you have any family that needs to be contacted tonight? I would rather you have company this evening."

Slight nods and blinks answered her back.

She would check back on them but after she gave a statement to the questioning police officer, who was already speaking to Élie Karsci.

"Did you get a good look at the woman's face that took you away?"

"Yes. I can describe her to you and perhaps do a sketch if you have some paper and a writing utensil."

The officer shook her head. "Let's wait on that. What did she want from you?"

Alex watched Élie as he stumbled over his words. "She wanted the combination for the safe, but I did not know it. She left empty-handed."

Alex looked hard at Élie, but either he did not see her or he pretended to not have her gaze. His face showed no emotion or tell of lying through his teeth.

The doctor checking Brookmeyer's pulse and her gunshot wound caught Alex's attention. She walked to Rueben's machine.

Cautiously, she examined the contraption as everyone stood over Brookmeyer's body. Her gaze went over the familiar brass and looked over the dominos and the tiny Ferris wheel. Behind it was something black and shiny that didn't blend as well against the brass—a gun. That wasn't there before. When did someone have the time to put it in and make it a part of the contraption without it being noticed?

Pierre didn't see this?

The only person capable would have to have engineering skill and be able to get into the airship without notice. Unfortunately, staff members from the school and Brookmeyer's own staff had access all the night before until just this evening.

"Ma'am?"

Alex jumped at the voice and turned.

A police officer.

"We need to speak with you about what happened tonight."

"Yes."

"You said there was a problem with the machine earlier?"

Alex nodded.

"How was it made to work again?"

"The engineers had been called into fix it." Alex's stomach rolled.

The police officer flipped through her notepad pages then stopped. "You said engineers?"

"Engineer. Mister Rueben, I mean. Mister Karsci was in his room."

The officer looked up at Alex. "So who helped him fix the machine?"

Alex's heart beat in her ears. She swallowed. If she lied, several witnesses would counter her words.

"My son. Madam Brookmeyer had asked for his help."

The officer's eyes narrowed. "Madam Brookmeyer asked an Anglo for assistance on this here complex contraption?"

Alex's spine stiffened.

"Is someone of his type licensed to operate or tinker with a machine?"

Time slowed, and Alex could not find the right words. There was a buzz in her head.

"No, but—"

"Ma'am, are you telling me that an unlicensed Anglo tinkered with a machine that killed one of the most respected philanthropists?"

"No. I mean, yes. I—"

The officer closed her notebook. "Right."

Alex watched the officer turn and make a beeline to Pierre.

The officer grabbed Pierre's wrist. "Sir, you are under arrest for operating a Class C machine without a license and under suspicion of the murder of Madam Brookmeyer."

Pierre looked at Alex in horror.

Alex heard the click of the handcuffs and the roar of her heartbeat in her ears. Alex followed the officer as she guided Pierre off the airship. Alex dare not try and touch the officer to get her attention for fear of being charged for assault.

Alex ran after Pierre, but a crowd of reporters began to block her pathway. She saw the officer put Pierre in the waiting carriage, his head down. He didn't look up once as his mother called his name.

Stopping, Alex remembered all her belongings were in the airship. She ran back inside and told Baxton that he was in charge of clean up.

"Tell Mr. G I will meet him at Maman Eloisa's!"

Several feet away from the airship was Pierre's little automobile. She didn't know how to drive or operate this contraption. Taking a moment to gather her bearings, she began running, trotting towards the police station.

It took over a half hour to reach the station. Alex's chef's coat was on her arm, but her undershirt was dripping in sweat.

"Officer," she called out. The woman turned, then her shoulders slumped.

"May I help you?"

"That's my son in there, when, I mean, how do I get him out of there?"

The officer tightened her lips. "I'm sorry ma'am, but unless you can prove he didn't murder Madam Brookmeyer, he's staying in there for a while."

"May I speak with him?"

"You have five minutes," the officer said.

Alex saw Pierre blinking back tears he did not want her to see in the dim light of the jail cell.

Pierre nodded. "The gun was not there when I helped fix the machine. Someone must have put it together."

"But how could they do it without anyone noticing?"

"The red-haired lady never got up during the entire meal. She only got up when Madam Brookmeyer had been..."

Alex thought for a moment.

"When the airship touched down and before the doctor got in, who was missing besides the red head?"

Pierre looked up in thought then finally said, "There was another photographer."

Flash!

"I never saw their face. They were under the drape to take the photograph. I think they were with—"

She struggled to remember the name. "Percival!"

"I remember them too! I don't think they were on the airship when we landed."

"Did the officers ask you any questions about this?"

Pierre shook his head.

"If they ask you anything, do not say a word. If you do, it may incriminate you. You working on the machine without a license is bad enough. I have to go speak with Guillaume and find a lawyer. I'll be back tomorrow morning, as soon as I can." She held his hand through the bars then let go and turned away.

Do not cry, she told herself.

Back at Maman Eloisa's, Alex prepared to give the well-thought-out explanation. "Maman," Alex began, but the words got caught in her throat.

Guillaume stepped forward.

"Guillaume just arrived and told me," Maman Eloisa said.

Alex hugged her mother. She felt Guillaume's hand resting on her shoulder.

"I went to the airship, and Baxton told me what happened. I went to the police station as soon as I heard, but you must have gone already. I spoke with Pierre and gave him some leftovers from the dinner."

"They think Pierre did it," was all she could manage to say.

Attempting to recall that evening's moment was narrow. Her memories of the murder and the events were like seeing through a tunnel, the outer rim surrounded by tufts of white cotton.

"I'll take care of Pierre," Guillaume offered. "You get some rest if you can tonight."

"Go and rest," her mother said before gently nudging her toward the stairs.

Alex didn't remember following orders, but she managed to undress her sleep-deprived body and felt herself drift off. But as easy as it seemed to fall asleep, the more difficult it was for her to escape the violent and gruesome dreams she had throughout the night.

Early the next morning, Alex rose, freshened up, and changed into trousers and a dress shirt. Once downstairs and in the kitchen, she threw an apron on and began baking the croissants she had prepped the evening of her arrival.

A batch of croissants that had been made for this morning's breakfast would not be eaten around the dining room table.

A moment that should have been she and Pierre regaling Maman Eloisa with stories about their once-in-a-lifetime moment cooking in an airship.

As Alex pushed the tray with the croissants into the pre-heated oven, she found her panic dissolving. It lessened more as each minute passed as she baked.

An hour later, with a small picnic satchel strapped to her hip, Alex strolled into the station.

"Officer Potkiss," Alex cheerily called out. "It is a beautiful day for some sweets, no?"

Officer Potkiss narrowed her eyes.

Alex ignored the suspicion and opened the box in front of the officer. "Freshly made."

The officer watched Alex unwrap the tissue paper to reveal croissants, blueberry muffins, crepes, and a little jar filled with chocolate sauce.

"Just a thank you for keeping my son safe last night and for allowing me to visit with him this morning."

Potkiss tried to protest, but Alex pushed the box into her hands and walked towards the jail area. "Through here, yes?"

She did not wait for an answer as Potkiss picked out a treat to devour.

"Pierre!" she whispered, spotting her son.

"Maman," he whispered back.

The other prisoners were asleep in other cells.

"Are you all right? Are you hurt? Have they kept you out of harm's way?"

"Maman, I am okay. Officer Meckelson and I have been playing chess whenever she comes in from patrol. She says I am quite the match."

Alex stroked her son's hair through the bars.

"Mr. G is calling his lawyer, and we hope to have them here by tomorrow. We will get you out."

"I know, maman."

"This was not how I hoped our fresh start would be. I am sorry."

Alex lifted her gaze, gathering her composure. She let out a long breath. "I have food for you."

"Ma'am, you cannot socialize with the prisoner without permission."

Alex turned to see Meckelson.

"Oh," Officer Meckelson said. The officer leaned in, a look of apology on her face. "Chef, I cannot let you stay too long, but—"

"I have a few crepes, croissants, and two blueberry muffins with the best streusel topping sitting with Officer Potkiss. I hope you will share with my boy."

Potkiss came strolling in with the box of treats. Meckelson peeled back the paper. Her eyes lit up, and she looked at Alex. "Oh I couldn't, chef."

Alex put up a hand. "I will not take them back, so you must accept my gift."

"Well, thank you. I will make sure Pierre gets some, but I'm sorry; you cannot be back here. If the chief found out—"

Alex put up her hand. "Say no more. I was never here. I am but a ghost."

Alex kissed his cheek through the bars and left.

Later that morning, she arrived back home, and Pierre's car was in Maman Eloisa's driveway. She guessed Guillaume must have driven it back, but her mind was too distracted to really care.

She walked into the house, greeted her mother with a kiss on the cheek, and took the apron her mother offered. They prepared several meals and desserts in silence. Both knew Alex would not eat any of it, and Maman Eloisa knew she would bring it to her welding club for dinner that night as they discussed technique and new project ideas.

To be free of Guardian Reid's ever-watchful eye and patronizing tone for the few days Alex and Pierre had travelled in their auto had been glorious.

Alex winced at the idea of having to hear Reid's lectures. It did not matter that Pierre was legally Alex's son. The fact that the two did not share blood would always be something of contention, and Reid was just a single representative of the Committee's bigotry.

In Reid's privileged mind, Pierre was Anglo and should not have been awarded use of advanced technology because surely he would use it for ill.

Alex imagined Guardian Reid's pursed lips as she would write her report of the errors of her charge Pierre, and probably encourage the Committee to terminate Pierre's legally earned licenses for using limited tech.

No way in Hades Alex would be able to sweet talk Guardian Reid to ignore correspondence with the Committee and keep the school from receiving bad press while trying to keep Pierre from going to prison. Alex needed help from people that would be able to help her find the killer and clear Pierre's name whilst keeping Reid from writing a biased report of the events.

Alex needed professionals.

"Sift this flour for me," Maman Eloisa said.

Alex did as her mother asked and helped make a large batch of gravy—enough for dinner that evening and more to be jarred.

Alex's thoughts fell back on her worries.

"Maman?" Alex said as the jars had cooled enough to put away.

Maman Eloisa put the last jar of gravy in the pantry when she answered. "Yes?"

"Eva's working a town away, but trying to reach her to ask for a favor is tricky."

Maman Eloisa let out a sigh.

"You know she has her own timetable to keep."

"True, but her having eyes and ears everywhere would help."

Eva's troupe was beyond skilled in that area, and Alex had seen it for herself.

Alex excused herself and used her mother's telegraphing system to dial the number of the only person she knew could help her and Pierre.

Eva Merchant, Ring Mistress of the Wicked Night Carnivale.

After she placed the message, Alex chose not to speak any more about it.

Just as she placed the apron back on, Maman Eloisa's telegraph chimed. Her mother answered it.

"Alex!"

Alex ran to her mother's side.

"It's Guillaume. His lawyer will be at the jail in a few minutes."

Ten minutes later, Alex and her mother set out for the police station. Maman Eloisa had cancelled her welding club meeting for that evening to support Alex.

A leather pouch was at Alex's hip filled with a care package of Lemon and Pearl tea cookies when she walked into the building.

The officer greeted the attorney, "Mrs. Darren! Good morning."

"Same to you," replied Mrs. Darren then made her way to her young client. "Mr. LeBeau, how are they treating you?"

Pierre stood up and shook his hand through the bars, "Well, ma'am."

"Pierre, I want you to tell me everything that you can remember about last night, and then we'll go from there."

The attorney was let into the cell with Pierre. Guillaume and Alex waited outside the cell and listened to Pierre.

"I had helped Madam Brookmeyer with the machine. After I had helped Élie, I mean, Mister Karsci, with the gadget, I went back to the kitchen to prep food for the dinner party."

Alex stepped back, away from the bars, and began eating one of her cookies made with the famous Pearl tea.

A tea otherwise known as Gunpowder due to its being hand-rolled into the shape of a gun pellet. When put in hot water, it would unfurl beautifully like a flower. Its taste was bitter, but the citrus brought out its complex flavor.

She hadn't meant to be ironic about the cookies, but the ingredients available to her just happened that way. She just hoped that her food would no longer have to be associated with misfortune. It had all started with that blasted Sea Salted Caramel ice cream when she came to Honfleur.

"Madam Reid must have the Committee already here by now," Guillaume said with a sneer.

"This is just something she and her cronies would love," she added. "I pray your friend can get Pierre out of this because we both know he didn't kill Brookmeyer."

Guillaume patted her hand then took a cookie. "I know. You do not deserve such hardship after what you went through with his father."

Alex drew in a sharp breath.

"Desolé," he said quickly. "I did not mean to bring up such pain."

Giving a weak smile, she bit into her cookie and waited quietly with Guillaume.

When the attorney was finished, she put his notes into her briefcase, shook Pierre's hand, and asked for the guard.

Then the attorney asked to speak with the chief. Meckelson guided the attorney to the chief's office, and Alex and Guillaume waited for over thirty minutes.

Alex watched Mrs. Darren shake the chief's hand.

"They will draw up the paperwork to release Pierre. They have no reason to keep him."

Alex blinked in surprise then dumbly handed the attorney a cookie.

"Thank you so much for all your help."

Attorney Darren just nodded and, with Guillaume behind her, walked out of the station.

Alex attempted to walk them out but bumped into someone.

"Oh, pardon."

Alex looked up to see not only Guardian Reid but someone almost as annoying standing alongside Reid.

"Ma'am, you have no say in these affairs. We will talk to your son," Guardian Reid said, moving past Alex and Maman Eloisa.

"Misses LeBeau," Alex corrected, following Reid and her assistant into the police station lobby.

"Not without his lawyer present," Alex continued. "The minute they made this into an investigation of technological crime, it involved the local law enforcement too. If you get to ask questions, then my son's lawyer and the law authorities get to ask full questions too."

"This isn't an interrogation."

"Then why do you need to question him without his attorney present?"

Maman Eloisa and Alex stood silent.

"You have no clue about how things change since it involves Madam Brookmeyer," Guardian Reid shot back.

"Is there something you'd like to tell us Miss, LeBeau?"

Alex looked to the voice asking the question. Standing beside Guardian Reid was her new assistant. Miss Laiton had asked the question.

Miss Laiton's fashion sense could be best described as a walking terrarium in a corset. Alex convinced herself that she did not prefer to dress up. Though if pressed to admit, it was sheer exhaustion keeping Alex from adorning herself in ostentatious clothing.

Alex raised an eyebrow at Miss Laiton, unamused. "What brings a botanist to a murder investigation?"

Miss Laiton smiled. "Well, greetings dear sister, it's wonderful to see you after such a long time."

CHAPTER 6

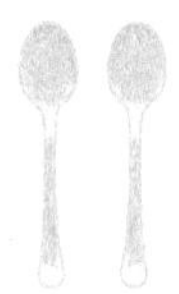

Maman Eloisa stepped forward. "Octavia, it is good to see you."

Miss Octavia Laiton smiled towards their mother.

Alex interjected. "Yes, too bad your visit includes spying on your nephew."

Octavia looked at Alex and grimaced.

Alex gave her sister a smug smile.

"Miss LeBeau, I do demand you speak to my assistant with a modicum of civility," Guardian Reid said.

Alex scowled at her sister. Out of the corner of her eye, Alex saw her mother throw her hands in the air as if forfeiting her chance to get involved with the rivalry.

"Yes, please do," Octavia chimed in.

Secretly, if Alex had been asked what she would wear, the answer would be hats decorated with tiny picnic or dinner scenes. Miniature faux picnic baskets with small blankets and tiny plates of food and desserts near the crown was a level of childlike whimsy that her career would not afford.

When did she stop creating? When did she stop liking to have fun?

The rhetorical question irritated her, and instead of taking the time to consider the answer, Alex decided to be petty and blame her sister for inadvertently making Alex ponder such questions in the first place.

Octavia continued talking, unaware that Alex was spinning scenarios in her head.

With each nod of her head, Octavia's plumed hat bobbed and swayed. How her sister kept her head from popping off with such overmuch decoration, Alex would never guess the secret.

"Sister, did you come to collect plant samples?" Alex pushed.

Octavia pushed the loupe in front of her empty eyeglass frame and leaned forward. "No," she replied. "I'm here to assist Guardian Reid while she is completing paperwork for another case."

Alex crossed her arms under her chest. "What would a botanist know of how to do Guardian Reid's job?"

Octavia let out a long sigh. "How are we to change their minds if we do not work from the inside? I am trying to better this establishment."

Silence.

"What are you doing besides complaining?"

Both women forgot Guardian Reid and Maman Eloisa's presence. In fact, they forgot everyone in the police station existed around them.

"Asking a question is now complaining?"

Octavia narrowed her eyes and straightened her spine. "I will be assisting in conducting an investigative search on Pierre's adherence to licensing protocol. I, I mean we, will answer any questions you may have about the process. Any findings, whether for or not in favor of Pierre, will be shared with Guardian Reid and the Licensing Board overseen by a branch of the Comm—"

Alex cut her off. "You may want to step in and try putting family first. Are you capable of such deeds?"

Octavia scowled, and her eyes said, "If you weren't my sister, I would fight you here and now."

Alex's vocal tone resembled what was often used when speaking to toddling children or condescending people to octogenarians. "Sister?"

Octavia's lips stayed shut in seething anger.

"Why could you not let Reid handle this?" Alex finally asked.

"I am looking out for you, Alex!"

"I do not need looking out for," Alex hissed back, ignoring how ridiculous it sounded saying in a police station.

Alex collected herself.

"I didn't want to be stuck in a laboratory all day every day. You are not the only one, dear sister, who can travel the world."

Alex laughed at Octavia. "You have not been farther than fifty miles from home until recently."

Even beneath her deep brown skin, Alex could see Octavia redden. "You will regret talking to me this way."

"Honestly, I regret talking to you now."

Octavia gasped, and for a moment, Alex thought her dramatic sister would swoon in front of her.

Alex drew herself close to her sister and looked her square in the eye. "He's not like Charles."

Octavia's eyes darted back and forth.

"He's your nephew. He will not turn out like Charles did."

Octavia's voice became low. "You do not know that."

Alex looked up into her sister's anger and now panic-stricken eyes. She reached for Octavia's hand, and for a moment Octavia stilled.

"It is in Pierre LeBeau's best interest that he cooperates," Guardian Reid cut in.

Alex noted her severe chestnut brown walking dress. The color reminded Alex of inferior quality chocolate and bad life choices.

Octavia pulled her hand away from Alex's.

If Alex had not known Octavia, she would believe the air of austerity was genuine, but she knew her naïve and misguided sibling well, so she was not impressed.

Alex rolled her eyes as Octavia flounced off in a huff. Well, her hat did most of the flouncing.

Octavia's intentions, though often honorable, always resulted in entropy. Her skills were best left to plant life, not people.

Alex turned her full attention to Guardian Reid.

"My son has and will cooperate. We are taking our leave as soon as the officers correct their mistake."

Guardian Reid set down her matching brown case and proceeded to unlatch it. "We can go over the licensing agreement you and he signed while we wait."

Alex eyed her up and down. "No need. I am up to date on the documents as I was the one who drafted them, and the Committee agreed to my terms only a few months ago. Now if you'll excuse me. I need to welcome my son home. It has been a trying experience especially for an innocent gentleman as himself."

"But Miss LeBeau—"

Alex stepped past Reid, and Reid attempted to get in front of Alex.

Attempted.

Maman Eloisa stepped in front of Reid with shoulders

back, eyes locked. Her intensity gained her a foot. "I believe my daughter has been clear as a bell. Good day, Miss," she emphasized the title.

In the jail area, Maman Eloisa was behind her. Reid had gone.

CHAPTER 7

Alex turned to her mother. "You see I did not do a thing to Octavia?"

Maman Eloisa waved a hand in her direction. Alex took the cue to drop the subject and address Officer Meckelson.

"Chef LeBeau, we will finish the paperwork in a few minutes, and then you can take your son home."

An hour later, Pierre, Alex, and Maman Eloisa left the station. Though the humidity was low and it was fully night, the heat was beyond blistering. In silence, Pierre and Alex walked through town on the way back home. A costermonger caught Alex's attention, and she stopped to sift through a few coins in her purse.

"What would you like?" she asked her mother and her son.

Behind tired eyes, Pierre's wearied mouth opened into a small smile before choosing the largest cluster of dark muscadine berries to eat. Maman Eloisa passed on the offer.

Paying the vendor, Alex hooked her arm through her son's elbow and continued walking back to the house. Pierre was too focused on eating the pulp out of the berries to notice Rueben Karsci walking to the building four doors away from them.

Many years ago, Alex had walked into the same establishment to chase the dragon for the first, and unbeknownst to her, the last, time. Unlike her friends, Alex found her body rejecting the opium and never went back with her friends, who became regular patrons.

"Alexandra?" Maman Eloisa asked, concern in her voice. "You all right?"

"Maman, what is it?" Pierre asked, his mouth semi-full of pulp, reminding her he was still a child in some ways.

"Nothing," Alex replied. "Nothing."

Once home, Alex unlatched the door, hooked her arm around her son's shoulders, and guided him into the foyer of her mother's house.

"I have some food for you once you get washed up," Maman Eloisa offered.

"There is no need."

Her mother looked back at Alex without blinking. Pierre's breath was low yet audible. The silence was so deafening Alex thought she heard her son blinking.

Ten long seconds passed between them. Then, "Pierre and I will be down in several minutes."

Maman Eloisa squeezed Alex's hand then leaned up to kiss Pierre on his forehead before turning back and going into the kitchen.

Alex had sent Pierre to bathe first as she laid out her change of clothes for the evening and that of the following day. A quick rap on her bedroom door stopped her from deciding between two sets of her best boots.

She opened her door. Pierre stood almost eye-to-eye with her.

Without a word, he barreled into her and hugged her, his

body shaking with sobs. His relief showed in every tear shed. She pulled his face to meet her, wiped his tears with her thumb. No words were spoken between them. There never needed to be after all the struggles they went through, but she said it anyways.

"My Pierre. You are home. No worries. Me and Maman Eloisa and your aunts will keep you safe. Always."

Pierre gave a weak smile then let out a long-held breath of relief.

She pulled him back into a hug so he would not see the tears in her own eyes. "It is all right. It is going to be all right," she whispered, but she was not sure if she was saying it for him or herself.

During her time in the bateau cast iron tub, Alex lingered far too long and lathered herself with vanilla-scented glycerin soap given as a goodbye gift from her friends in New Virginia less than a year ago.

Somehow in her brief time in the tiny coal town, someone had discovered she loved to smell like food. Flowers made her sneeze or worse, lavender made her nauseous, but food was comforting. When Pierre was but a toddler, he grabbed Alex's face in his chubby hands and told her, "You smell warm, like cookies."

As odd and awkward as it would look to an outsider, Alex took joy in that moment and always made sure to smell of something familiar, motherly. In all those years, she never changed to a different perfume or scent. The power of scent could comfort or upset.

While her identity was not wrapped in one title, she did take joy in knowing that she had been graced with a gift of becoming Pierre's mother.

Despite the circumstances that kept surrounding them, Pierre always found his way back home. She had grown beyond worried he would begin to fear travelling. The past year had been a test of her strength and faith, but Pierre had never ceased being gentle-hearted. In all that they had suffered, she was grateful he had not grown cynical at such a youthful age.

As the water drained from the bath, Alex stood and dried herself off. The last remains of warm water loudly left the tub. She wrapped the towel around her, grabbed the bucket of ice, sat on the rim of the tub before pouring the ice onto her warm feet.

She closed her eyes and enjoyed the reprieve from the swelling in her feet. Only when she felt herself shivering in the warm room did she step out of the tub and dry her feet before changing into clean clothes. She soon fell asleep.

The next morning, she regretted being too lazy the night before to wash and set her hair. Quickly, she applied witch hazel at her scalp, massaged it in, and placed her hair into a presentable bun before walking down the back stairs into the kitchen.

"Morning, maman."

Maman Eloisa raised an eyebrow then continued to sip her chicory coffee. Alex would never understand why her mother drank such when Louisiana was providing delicious, real coffee.

Alex had once lectured her mother on the benefits of uncut coffee. The exchange resulted in Maman Eloisa calling Alex a "gastronomic prig" that should keep her food opinions to herself.

Maman's words had stung. Years later when Alex became an instructor, she got to observe firsthand how arrogant first-year cooking students could be. A harsh mirror for Alex.

"Alexandra? Is all this police business behind you?" Maman Eloisa asked as Alex came through the passageway.

She froze. "Not sure. Élie told the police that the murderer got away empty handed, but I saw him hand her something before she jumped out of the airship. I think Élie is hiding—"

"You need to leave things alone and mind your own business. Let the police do their job, and you do yours. Always meddlin'."

Alex clenched her jaw.

"Now you know that your sister Octavia is trying to make a name for herself. I am not fond of Reid either or her determination to take away Pierre's chance to make something more of his life."

Alex's facial features began to soften. "I—"

Maman Eloisa put up a hand, and Alex closed her mouth. "Now, I will give you and she a tissue for your issue so y'all can get to resolving it. Because frankly, you are getting on my damn nerves!"

Alex gasped and caught Pierre smirking before he buried his face in the plate of food in front of him.

Her mother handed her a plate of food.

She wants you safe. She's speaking from wanting her child safe, Alex told herself as she sat in the chair opposite of Pierre at the other end of the long, wooden table.

For whatever the reason, Maman Eloisa spoke no more on the topic. Such was her way. When she opened her mouth to speak, you listened. You did not talk back or give an explanation. If she didn't ask you for your input, then you did not give it.

Once when Alex was a young girl of eleven, she overheard a man giving her maman a reason to something she didn't ask on. After that one-sided exchange of maman putting him in his place all without raising her voice, she never saw the man speak back to her mother except for cordial interaction.

The electric doorbell that Mr. G had installed for her mother rang.

"Better not be those kids from down the road again," Madam Eloisa said and put down her café au lait.

When her mother left the room, Alex picked up the cup of coffee.

"You betta put my coffee down," her mother called from the hallway leading to the front door.

Alex did as she was told.

"It's about time you came by after being in town for several days, young lady."

"Maman," came Octavia's voice.

Alex walked to the front door to observe the chastising of her sister in person.

CHAPTER 8

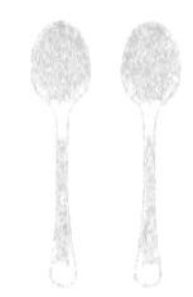

Maman Eloisa joined Alex, and they moved to the porch chair, forgetting to close the front door in the excitement.

"Sister," Alex said in Octavia's direction. "I figured that when Pierre had been falsely arrested days ago, you would have reached out to Maman. To apologize for being involved with the potential investigation of your nephew."

Maman Eloisa looked from Alex to Octavia, awaiting a reply. Annoyance flashed behind Octavia's eyes at her sister.

"Maman, this is the first time I was able to step away. I was tirelessly working to keep peace between Guardian Reid and," she looked at Alex, "Pierre. Besides, I was tied to the electro-telegraph for several days to make sure all charges were dropped. He has been through so much that the idea of him in that cell for another day was something I could not stand."

Alex would need hip waders. Surely her mother did not believe the bullmalarky rolling off her sister's tongue.

Octavia hugged their mother and stuck out her tongue to Alex, making her giggle.

All the years of effort to keep Octavia away from the Committee did not stick. Alex knew there was no way to convince Octavia that everyone came in to the Committee with ideals. The problem was when reality showed the complexity of their America. It was an America whose utopia was flawed—flawed in a manner that was subtle, long-reaching, and filled with a danger Alex did not want Octavia to ever discover.

"I see everything is the same since I was last here."

Octavia released their mother, and Alex spun around to face Eva. Eva wore a bright red-and-white-striped coat and skirt with a small, white top hat jauntily angled off center of her head.

Anyone else would be melted, but not Eva. Always the show woman, Eva never had a hair out of place and looked ready for a grand party. For a woman that led a clandestine group, Eva sure did bring attention to herself. Unlike their sister Octavia, Eva was one hell of an actress when needed but preferred the truth over omitting parts of a story. No secret. Eva was Alex's favorite sister.

Maman Eloisa practically pushed Octavia away and ran to Eva.

"Where have you been?" she asked as she hugged her red-striped daughter. "All that travelling with them carnival folks and you not once thought to send me a postcard?"

"Well, I am here now, maman."

"It only took a murder and your poor nephew to bring you back home."

"But I am home now, maman, so embrace it before it is gone like Alex's Maple Pecan Popcorn."

Their mother squeezed Eva tighter then, "Eva. You did not bring any of them around. They must be starving. No one should live on carnival food."

Eva pulled back. "They are asleep. It was a long night."

Maman Eloisa put up a hand in understanding. "Say no more. Now come and have a seat. Octavia, move so your sister doesn't mess up that beautiful dress of hers."

Octavia's mouth dropped open, but she did as she was told.

As was the nature of things. Whichever child had been away the longest received the most doting on. Eva's choice in work kept her travelling, so for as long as Alex could remember, Eva always won their maman's attention when visiting.

They may have had over thirty birthdays together, but all three sisters went out of their way to annoy the others.

It was an unspoken game they all played, and no one's feelings were ever truly hurt by it.

Well, besides the trouble between Octavia and Alex.

"I'd love to stay and chat, but I have to be at the cookery." Alex said her pleasantries, kissed their mother goodbye, and headed to the school with Pierre at her side.

"Maman, stop staring at me. It is not like I am the dead come back to life."

Alex ignored him.

Pierre rolled his eyes and continued walking alongside his mother. "You must promise to stop when we get to the school."

Begrudgingly, Alex nodded her agreement. No student needed to believe she was playing favorites.

Before they reached the entrance, Alex mentally prepared all the ways she could divert any questions about the last several nights. Along with trying to push out the nagging thought of why Élie had lied about giving items to Furious Angel.

The police officers seemed to be unaware of the exchange and that did not sit right with Alex.

She came into her class with the students paying attention

to prepping their mise en place, not her entrance. Pierre fell in line.

"Morning chef!" a voice behind her called from the pantry.

Alex looked inside to see Mr. Jones gathering leaveners from the shelf.

Another shriek came from the freezer. The remaining students and Alex went to the sound to find Baxton holding a hanger with the crook of his finger with a perfectly preserved frozen chef's coat.

There were snickers and Alex suppressed a chuckle. "Go grab one of the extra coats that are near Monsieur G's office, and hang that frozen one outside to thaw. If there are any other pranks to discover, I recommend you do so now because I will not be stopping class to coddle you. Do I make myself clear?"

"Yes, chef!" the students said at once.

"Good. Class in five minutes upstairs!"

As she awaited their arrival, she set to teach her students how to work with tin-plated steel rings.

Alex wandered to the front of the classroom and passed by the row of iron-framed desks that were bolted to the floor.

Each desk had been repurposed from an abandoned town's school and still had a circular notch at the top of the desk for old inkwells for dipping pens in.

Tiered levels held desks along the back wall to give each student a clear view of the chef instructor. They were long, wooden tables with swing-arm, leather-cushioned seats tucked under.

"As most of you are aware, Madam Brookmeyer was murdered during the airship dinner."

The students attempted to look as if they had not been swimming in or passing gossip about the incident that morning.

"For the next ten minutes, I will answer as many questions about last night that I can. After that, any queries, concerns, or the need of students, especially those working the event, may come to me. If you are worried but would rather arrange a time to chat in private, please leave me a note."

The students didn't say a word.

Alex anticipated being bombarded with notes later that afternoon. "Chef?"

"Yes, Davian."

"Is this going to get the school shut down?"

"We have not done anything wrong."

"What I think he means is, will the school get blamed for it? Will Mr. G have to shut down the school if attendance wanes?"

Alex nodded, understanding. "Good question. I do not think so. Newspapers report facts, and there is no reason the school would be associated with or tied to the murder."

"But Sunday's paper mentioned you and the school by name along with Madam Brookmeyer's murder. And today—"

Alex kept her expression neutral as Ren spoke, rolling her wheelchair forward. Alex mistakenly thought the students would need consoling for their emotional well-being, and they were worried about the future of their school.

Alex's mind came back from wandering. Ren had stopped talking.

"At this time, no one has been charged. Police do have a few suspects, and I'm happy to say no one at this school, nor the school itself, is on that list."

"That's not what the newspaper hinted at this morning. They mentioned that Madam Brookmeyer's machine she was going to reveal is now missing from the Damask Hangar. It also mentions Chef Heston's abrupt departure and now Madam Brookmeyer to be a sign that Mr. G is not someone to do business with."

"Mr. G's reputation speaks for itself. For now, I believe it best to remind yourself of what brought you to this school in the first place. I will never tell you what you should do or whom to believe. I do hope you believe your peers who were at the event and know that none of us would ever put ourselves, or the school, in jeopardy. Okay?"

The students seemed to take comfort in her words. Though to Alex's annoyance, worry about the school's reputation began to simmer at the back of her head.

Élie lying to the police officer about giving items to the Furious Angel did not squelch it. She had tried to stay out of it, telling herself that Élie would cooperate with the officers. She could not force Élie to tell them, and if she mentioned it to the officers, would they believe her? Or would the officers think she was trying to pin things on Élie in an attempt at revenge?

By the end of the afternoon session, Alex's anxiety had worsened like water on a grease fire.

To distract her from her thoughts, Alex began a refresher lesson on yeast in the form of muffins.

Sweet English muffins with saffron and cardamom-poached pears were today's dessert for the restaurant. The students were vocal about their unease of the strong yet subtle flavors combined.

What did saffron taste like since it was usually put in rice?

During the demo class, Alex pushed the topic and pushed the students to think of the expensive spice as something more than a one-trick pony in cuisine.

"Honey. If you have the right type, saffron tastes like honey," Alex replied as she stirred the simple syrup. She had one of the students roll over one of the cardamom seeds with a rolling pin to release the distinctive fragrance then pass it around for everyone to smell.

"As you can smell, a little is all you need. If you ever get a chance to taste Chai, which means tea in Hindi and Hebrew, you will taste this cardamom, cinnamon, and other spices.

"Chai," she continued, "is from India. This spiced black tea is generally drunk with milk and is very sweet and delicious. You must travel abroad to really understand what it is you are making now. We can make all the foods from around the world, but until you taste them for yourself in their respective countries, you will feel as if something is missing in your chef's bag of tricks."

"Chef?" one of the students asked. "What does Chai taste like?"

Alex looked up and smiled. "It tastes like Christmas."

The students were instructed to let the pears sit in a bowl of cardamom and saffron syrup while they made the sweet English muffins.

Once again, Alex checked each student's progress. Her attention fell onto Baxton.

"A lot of folks cannot bake, or they do not like it. You wanna know why?"

Baxton grimaced, skeptical.

"It's precise. It's mathematical. It's chemistry. It is edible science, but you Baxton, you understand how things react and why."

Baxton shook his head. "I don't know the history of things like Mr. Jones."

"History is not chemistry. Everything you make comes out exactly as the recipe tells you it should, but what if the recipe is wrong? How would you keep from creating a dish you cannot eat?"

"I look at the recipe," he replied, his tone inferring it a fool's query.

Alex nodded in agreement. "I think you could figure it out by smell. I think you've made these recipes so many times and perfected them that you could probably create them without measuring the ingredients. In fact," she paused for effect, "I think you could create some interesting desserts with flavors that are tried and true with a hint of surprise."

He shook his head. "I wouldn't even know where to start."

"Don't. Just play. You have this entire school and the pantries whose contents are available to you. This is an opportunity for you to discover new things. Have fun. It's only food."

Baxton's eyes grew wide. "But what if certain ingredients are off limits to students like the saffron that's so hard to come by?"

"True, true. How about this; you draft a recipe and show it to me or Mr. G, and if we sign off on the ingredients, you can experiment in one of the kitchens when class is not in session. Fair?"

Baxton offered his hand in a gentleman's agreement.

When all the students completed their desserts, Alex had them make a whipped cream to go in between the sliced muffin and quarter-inch sliced pears then encouraged everyone to taste their creation.

With the evidence eaten, the students tidied up their stations, walked through the foyer, and went up the stairs to gather their belongings. "See you tomorrow, chef," many students said in passing.

Except for one student.

"Pierre?"

"Yes, chef," he answered but didn't cease washing the dishes.

Alex lowered her voice. "Tell Maman Eloisa I will be home late. I have an errand to run."

"What kind of errand?" Pierre asked.

"Personal. Now mind your business, and get home. I don't want to hear from your granmère that you got sidetracked. I finally have you home again."

A good chef gets to know their surroundings, Alex told herself as she walked out of the front entrance. Class was over, which meant Josephine was free.

Josephine was nowhere to be seen.

Disappointed, Alex took it upon herself to examine the rows of herbs in the raised garden bed. Nary a weed found in the rich bed of soil.

Small, wooden markers stood proud beside each flourishing plant, but the words inscribed didn't seem to use English as an identifier. The letters were in English but rearranged with odd accents Alex could not comprehend.

"Gaelic."

Alex stood straight and looked beside her.

Josephine.

Alex tried to not smile so broadly but failed. "Is that what you speak?"

Josephine gave a curt nod.

Something new. Josephine was not only someone new but Alex found she was always learning something new.

"Are you ready for the tour?"

Alex hesitated. "I have to check on something. I have an errand."

"Would you like a truncated version or the lesson I give our first-year students?"

Despite herself, Alex eagerly nodded. "I have time for a full lesson."

Josephine's eyes glittered. She took a deep breath and began.

"The difference between a potager and a garden is that one can serve dual purpose. That is what a potager can do. It is both ornamental and functional for the chef's needs. When sitting down to sketch a garden plan, I consider the chef and their needs."

Alex shifted from swooning to genuine focus on Josephine's lesson.

"When designing such a garden, you do best to have an ornamental focal point. Remember, we are balancing function with beauty. For me, I love the trellis because they are a doorway of sorts, but you Chef Alex, you can choose whatever else you would like. You can choose a stone, a reflection globe, or anything else your heart can imagine."

Josephine made gardening sound like magic.

"As a chef, you have certain vegetables and herbs you repetitively use, so you would place them in their potager, but you don't put them all in one bed. In a potager, you would put an array of the same items in different garden beds while keeping it balanced."

They strolled around the first garden that faced west then made their way to the eastern side.

"A good gardener knows how to use plants to repel pests while making the garden look beautiful. Though I must say it is difficult to do if one of the pests prefers to eat your repellant and the budding leafy green of your carrot tops," Josephine added.

Alex found herself getting a thrill over Josephine's irritation about the pest. Clearly, Josephine was not truly angry. Her being peeved about nature was charming.

"Over here, I used the overhang of this wee kumquat tree's shade for the herbs and vegetables that do well out of direct sunlight. Though just like the west garden, I use color variants; in the east, there are bolder colors to counter the shade."

Alex squinted. Stepped back. Squinted. Tilted her head then squinted again at the garden.

"Oh," she said. Her head righted, and her eyes widened. "How utterly clever!"

Josephine had arranged the garden bed to look like a

square with each corner rounded. Alex squinted her eyes to figure the pattern.

"Shield knot," Josephine supplied.

"Does it have a meaning?"

"Protection. To ward off evil. You know, slugs."

Alex chuckled.

A spot caught Alex's eye. She turned her head. Just a shadow from one of the trees. The air shifted as the wind blew, the branches swayed and waved slightly, shifting the sunlight across the grass. The shadow stayed stationary.

Alex focused. The shadow was rounded and breathing.

"Oh," she gasped quietly.

"What?" Josephine asked then looked to see where Alex was looking.

Alex pointed. "A lapin!" she whispered.

Under the low-hanging branch of the oak tree was a small, black rabbit. Its body quickly expanded and contracted with its quick breaths, and its tiny, black nose wiggled.

"Ah," Josephine called out. "You found the Pest."

"Oh no. It is too cute to be a pest."

Josephine snorted in protest. "You haven't had your vegetables be consumed overnight by such a nuisance."

"A cute nuisance," Alex corrected. "It's hungry. Look at how tiny it is."

Josephine was not convinced.

Alex was overwhelmingly consumed with the need to scoop it up and pet it.

"Where are you going?" Alex heard behind her as she walked forward.

"To pet the bunny," she replied then realized that the response could be taken as a euphemism. She decided to not follow that trail of thought and once again decided that it was all Josephine's fault for starting it.

"You are not going to be able to catch it."

Alex kept walking forward towards the somewhat still pitch-black creature. It kept eating, and though never moving, she was convinced that the rabbit was watching Alex with each step.

Only a few feet away, the rabbit's nose stopped twitching.

She slowed her walking to a stand then bent at the knees and began calling to it as if it were a dog.

She made kissing noises with her lips, stuck out her arm, pinched her fingers together and rubbed the tips back and forth to call attention to the rabbit. It did not budge.

"So," Josephine whispered in her ear. "What are you going to do with it when you catch it?"

Alex had been so focused on the creature she had not heard Josephine move towards her. Though it startled her, Josephine's warm breath on her ear was all too pleasant and, dare Alex say, welcomed.

Alex gave a hard swallow. "I had not thought that far ahead."

Josephine's low chuckle near her ear. Alex licked her lips.

"Chef Alex, remember that you are at a cooking school. There is only one outcome to this situation."

Alex grimaced, her bottom lip jutting out like a petulant child. She raised her voice. "Not if I can help it."

The rabbit hopped away.

Alex turned to face Josephine. Their faces only inches from one another. Josephine looked too amused at Alex's desire to save the rabbit.

"It's not funny."

Josephine said nothing but nodded in playful, condescending agreement. "Oh yes. A serious matter."

Alex rolled her shoulders back. "You," she said through a tight jaw. "You are...you are... Well I do not have the right word for what you are right now."

Josephine let out a laugh. "Chef Alex, *you* are somethin', you know that, right?"

If there was a visual for what Josephine's laugh and smile did to her, it would be a puddle. Josephine made Alex feel like a roll of compound butter melting in the sun.

"Stop it! Go back to talking about plants. You are less annoying to me when you talk of gardens."

Josephine smiled and walked towards the eastern garden bed. Alex walked only inches away from her, their foot falls matching in time.

Right, left, right.

"I have a question for you," Josephine said.

Don't smile.

"Would you come with me to—"

"Yes!" Alex felt her cheeks grow hot. Josephine tilted her head back and laughed. "I am so sorry. Continue."

"Miss LeBeau—"

"Call me Alex."

"Miss Alex—"

"No, just Alex."

Josephine sighed in mock annoyance. "Just Alex."

"May I share something with you?"

Josephine nodded.

"I am worried about Guillaume. Well, his school's reputation."

"Aye, that has been my burden as well as of late."

Alex looked at Josephine. "Oh."

"What he has done here means a lot to many people. I don't know what I would do if this was taken away."

Alex contemplated Josephine's words before saying, "I think there may be something the police officers missed the other night when they detained Pierre. Something that Élie Karsci didn't tell the police."

Josephine looked at her, not comprehending.

"Élie told the police that the murderer got away empty-handed, but he handed her something before she jumped out of the airship. I think Élie is hiding something."

Josephine's eyes widened. "Do you think he had a hand in killing Madam Brookmeyer? Maybe you should tell the police officers."

"Maybe. Though I'm worried that they will not take it seriously. One must admit that it would look as if I was finger pointing and attempting revenge if I went to them now."

Josephine nodded in understanding.

"Josephine, I won't know until I can shake off the feeling that Madam Brookmeyer may have something that could point a finger at him."

"What do you think it could be?"

"Blueprints. I was thinking about the night of the dinner and how the questions to Brookmeyer were about a new invention. It sounded like something that would help the community. I cannot ask Élie for insight, and I do not think Rueben, Mr. Ormont, is able to stand, let alone carry a conversation on the subject."

"Well, that does sound like a problem," Josephine said.

"I think the blueprints that the killer was looking for may be somewhere in Madam Brookmeyer's residence. I have this feeling that Élie may have given Furious Angel—the murderer—a fake."

"Or maybe there's no blueprint but something else Élie may be hiding," Josephine supplied.

"Oh, that is a good point."

"So what happens if we find new evidence?"

"We can bring it to them."

Josephine watched her for a moment. "You are the most..." She shook her head. "If we get into trouble, I am blaming you."

"Fair," Alex replied. "It's just a hunch. You don't have to

come. It is dangerous and not polite to ask you to do something possibly illegal."

"I'm in!"

Alex was ecstatic and slightly caught off guard by Josephine's enthusiasm for doing something nefarious.

"I don't get out much," Josephine explained.

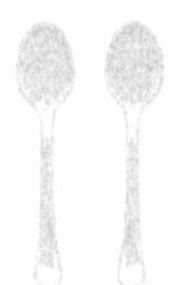

CHAPTER 9

Meanwhile, Pierre walked along the apartments on the opposite side of town. They stood close to one another with symmetry and colorful paint. He smiled, remembering the first time he made a gingerbread house. When Pierre was younger, his mother decided to craft a gingerbread house for the holidays.

With piping bag ready next to the bowl of white royal icing, Pierre was ready to construct a small, brown house like his friends and their families had done and put on display.

His mother made him mix colors into separate bowls holding similar portions of the edible glue then showed him how to fill in the gingerbread walls with muted colors. Once dry, they piped flowers and embellishments, and he was bored.

As beautiful as the finished gingerbread house they had created together was, Pierre would have been happy to pipe copious amounts of white icing at the cookie wall edges and decorate with a chaotic array of candies.

His mother did try to engage him in less techno activities for his own safety, but when he was tall enough to reach the pedals of the automobile that had been left in his mother's care, for reasons she refused to speak on, she gave in. In his excitement, he told his mother she would never regret allowing him his first license to operate basic technology.

Pierre pressed the doorbell, followed by footsteps.

"Yes?" Mr. Élie said, opening the door.

Pierre drew the small moleskin notebook from his satchel. "You dropped this the other evening," he said.

Élie looked at the hand thrust in front of him. Understanding fell over his eyes. "I did not remember dropping it. There was so much...I mean, it was difficult to focus."

Pierre nodded in understanding.

"I-I did not open it. I mean, I opened the first pages to figure out who it belonged to, but that is all."

Élie took the book. "I wouldn't tell anyone if you had read it from front to back."

Pierre looked up from his feet and into Élie's eyes, decoding his words.

"Knowledge should be available for all. It is up to each individual to use it wisely."

"I do," Pierre said. "I mean, I try. I can only do so much with the license I have, though one day, I hope to do what you and Mr. Rueben do."

Élie did not speak. Glanced around at the surroundings, "It is best not to further this conversation outside. Would you like a cup of tea?"

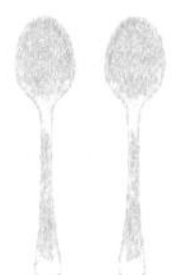

CHAPTER 10

Alex had assumed she and Josephine would use the dark cover of night to get in and out of Brookmeyer's summer residence. Unfortunately, they were deterred by the town's anticipated fireworks celebration.

"Out of all the nights," Josephine said.

Alex nodded her head.

While nervous at how it had been too easy to recruit Josephine to help her search for blueprints, Alex could sense that the Scottish woman felt helpless over Guillaume's plight too.

"So how will we get in?" Josephine asked as they stood at the front entrance.

Alex crouched down, looked up at Josephine before pulling out her tiny toolset. She picked the lock. She put her hand on the knob, and a scream came from behind the door in the house.

The screams grew louder until she opened the door and could see in the light of a low gas lamp the assailant was kicking the maid while she curled on the ground.

Alex didn't think but ran and barreled into the first

assailant and began using her fist against his face. Her blows sure and violent, her mind no longer in a place of logic. Instead, Alex was protecting someone other than herself because the maid was helpless. Alex's anger raged on as she took it out on the maid's attacker.

She hadn't noticed that she had knocked him out, but a second came forward.

Alex looked around for the kitchen knives and grabbed one from the magnetic strip on the wall near the stove.

The intruder regained his composure and held his own blade in his hand. Alex looked him square in the eye and waited for him to make his move.

He lunged at her, and she turned sideways and made a shallow slice at his kidney area. He reached a hand out to cover his wound. His eyes were full of surprise. Alex was certain she would take him down if necessary, but she needed information, not a fight to the death.

He turned and lunged toward her again, and she blocked the blade by contacting her wrist with his and made another shallow cut. His eyes showed fear and confusion. Whatever he did, she countered it and made a punishing, shallow cut to the offending area.

Her movements were minimal and quick. And her opponents were predictable, sloppy. He had been hired for something, but it was obvious that using weaponry wasn't normal for him. He used the blade to provoke fear and nothing else. Alex knew knives all too well, and she knew that a stab to the femoral artery could end this fight in less than two minutes. But she wasn't that way anymore.

She dropped the knife and attacked him and disarmed him in a flash by breaking his wrist. He sucked air in through his teeth then let out a yelp when she held onto the wounded wrist.

She turned around to see the first had regained consciousness. He jumped on Josephine's back as she was checking on the maid. Before Alex could attempt to help, Josephine went back to the first fight and threw punches like a trained boxer, never staying still, moving and being so swift that Alex was shocked and impressed.

She was so impressed that she was not prepared for the sucker punch of a third assailant's good fist. Alex got a glimpse of the third's blonde hair before she went down.

Alex opened her eyes and found Josephine's dark eyes looking down at her. "She's gettin' away," she managed to croak out.

Alex's left shoulder blade ached. She grimaced as she rolled it to hinder any growing stiffness the following day...it was painful, but from past fights, Alex had learned it necessary.

"I tied up the one with the broken wrist with a lamp cord. She got me in my ribs. That's going to smart in the mornin'," Josephine said, reaching her bare forearm out.

Alex took it. Both women stood; Alex righted her high shirt collar and sprinted out the front door and down the wooden steps.

"And just where are you going now?" Josephine called out from behind her.

"To find that blonde!"

The Scottish gentlewoman caught up to her and turned her around. "Ma'am, with respect, I say that the cheese has slid off your cracker. Respectfully."

Alex looked over her shoulder. "She is getting away."

Josephine tapped her shoulder.

Alex brought half her attention back to the Scottish woman before her. Even as the sun had deeply set on the moonless night, Alex watched as the lamp light flickered against Josephine's sard-hued skin. Josephine could be quite distracting at the most inconvenient times.

"We can find another way."

"Perhaps, but—" Alex glanced over her shoulder again to see another woman from Brookmeyer's house chasing behind someone amongst the crowd. Furious Angel darted around the bottlebrush tree.

"There's more than one," Josephine said with surprise.

"I see her!" Alex exclaimed. "I'd recognize that under-cooked, shortbread-colored hair anywhere. Come on."

Josephine made a yelp as Alex grabbed her by the hand and ran.

The night was not as scorching hot as Singapore in July, but the humidity was worse. Running and weaving through the strolling crowd felt as if she were running in water, possibly breathing it too.

Is this what fish experienced?

Alex kept her eye on the bolting figure ahead of them moving around the shadows and hedges. The humidity kept the scent of grilled peaches and sugar hanging in the air near the center of the green of Honfleur. The Furious Angel was heading towards the white sand beach.

Good gravy, not the water.

As many skills as she had acquired, Alex had never learned to swim well. The irony that she preferred to live near bodies of water because of familial traditions was not lost on her.

"Ma'am!" Josephine called out to a nearby officer. "We need your assistance."

Josephine kept running, and Alex bee-lined for the officer as well. "Yes. Do hurry," she added as she followed behind Josephine, who was chasing after Furious Angel.

Gas lamplight glinted off the multiple buttons along the sides of her soft, leather shoes as they pounded on the pavement. She stumbled as cobbled ground became sand and tufts of greenery. Later, Alex would recall later that running on sand while wearing shoes was not her best idea.

Where were the Furious Angel and her lackey headed?

The observation tower stood behind them and the Marmalade pier a few feet ahead, then nothing.

Alex struggled to run on the loose sand and evade running into stationary night picnickers.

Dodging a citizen, she moved towards the water and welcomed the compacted sand underneath her feet. Her steps were true with longer strides as she looked ahead, keeping her gaze on the blonde and the netted, buoyant dome peeking from over the smattering of trees. The Furious Angel was headed right for it beyond the plethora of oaks, but Alex lost sight of the assistant.

Alex glanced over her shoulder to see the lean Josephine keeping up. Josephine gave a quick point of her fingers to the far right of the Furious Angel before following the figure running into the trees.

Once she caught up to the blonde, Alex had no plan, and from the previous encounter, it could prove deadly for her, but worse, for Josephine. She strayed to the middle then abruptly veered to the left.

The crowds along the beach lessened, but a few people were sitting on picnic blankets, in awe of a newly purchased item. Alex spotted the sivakasi firework, snatched it before the people could protest, and kept running.

"Desolé," she called behind her.

All she needed was the miniature Dobereiner's lamp that was safely tucked in Josephine's sporran.

Her breath was too labored to groan as she disappeared into the forest.

The blood flow was particularly strong at her temples, at the bump on her head. It throbbed with each heartbeat. Her discomfort, that the Furious Angel was the direct cause of it, and the riding up of her undergarments after running further irritated Alex.

In an unladylike manner, she removed the fabric from the crack of her posterior.

The hot air balloon barely shifted from its tether. Amber glass jugs sat close by one of the anchoring hooks, one see-through and the other solid. Most likely each filled with sulfuric acid and the other filled with iron shavings.

The Furious Angel untethered the ropes on opposite sides.

The sounds of a scuffle came from the right of the trees. The assistant tumbled out, skidding on his back to a stop a few feet from the acid and shavings. Josephine stepped out from the shadows, her hands still balled into fists. Alex would never need to concern herself with the potager's wellbeing.

Alex looked back to the balloon. The blonde kept untying the ropes except for the last one, grabbed the gallon jugs, and hoisted them into the gondola basket.

How could she not hear the assistant?

Alex ran to Josephine.

The Furious Angel looked back at the scene. The face held a stubble jaw line and offset nose wearing a blonde wig. That was not Furious Angel.

They had chased a decoy.

The decoy smiled, and the third assistant, who was on the ground, was laughing.

At least the one with the broken wrist was still at Brook-meyer's house.

Dread washed over Alex. They had left the poor maid alone with him!

Later at the Honfleur Police Station, Alex sat on the hard wooden bench. The unwelcoming seat kept her awake as she waited for Josephine to give her statement of the night's events.

It never occurred to Alex that anyone would be working with or for the Furious Angel. The confirmation of this simultaneously scared her and gave her relief. Working solo meant she'd most likely to have a dead trail. The more people assisting Furious Angel, the more leads there would be.

Now the question was not who they were but what purpose did they serve besides throwing pursuers like the police off the Furious Angel's scent?

Alex had no clout nor business to be in a room while the officers questioned the others, so she had no way to get more information.

What she could deduce was that they were after something Furious Angel needed, and it was valuable enough to pull off this ruse.

Josephine came out of the questioning room and sat on the bench.

After sitting in silence on the hard bench for over seventy-five minutes, Alex & Josephine were informed that the maid was going to be fine, but the assailant with double broken wrists was not able to say the same.

"Double broken? But I only br—"

Josephine elbowed Alex in the ribs. Alex promptly shut her mouth.

"The maid, why was she there at Madam Brookmeyer's home?" Alex asked.

"She was gathering her things when several men broke into the house. Said they were looking for blueprints before one hit her and knocked her out," the officer replied then grimaced. "Why am I telling you?"

Wide-eyed, Alex shrugged.

There would come a time that she would not get away with looking so innocent, but today was not that day. Though in her mid-thirties, Alex just had a face that made people spill their secrets. Who was she to not utilize that gift for gathering information to help her friend?

As both women patiently waited, the evening brought in multiple townsfolk with a range of minor to disorderly types of incidents.

Was it the fireworks? The summer season? The sweet alcoholic beverages that brought out the need for citizens to make sure officers earned their pay?

Josephine was given permission to leave the station, and an officer offered to drive her home.

"No, thank you. I need to clear my head. I'm going to walk," Josephine replied to the officer then nodded her head in Alex's direction before wishing her a good evening.

Josephine parted ways with Alex with only a quiet goodbye. It went without saying that walking one another home was not the best of ideas that evening.

Alex stayed back for a few minutes to give Josephine enough lead time.

Élie stepped into the department looking dazed.

"Mister Karsci. What are you doing here?" Alex asked from the bench.

Élie looked in her direction, his eyes not recognizing her face.

"From the airship dinner," she supplied.

His eyes lit with recognition. "Chef LeBeau. How did you get here so fast? How did you know?"

"Know what?"

Panic flashed behind his eyes.

"Mr. Karsci?" Officer Meckelson called out.

Élie turned his attention to the officer and crossed to her.

"Officer..." Élie searched for the nametag on the chest. "Officer Meckelson. Rueben has gone missing. I believe he's in danger."

Officer Meckelson put up a hand. "Reuben Ormond? Have you spoken to any officer on duty about this yet?"

"No, I do not know where he could be, but Chef LeBeau's son is all right. He's with me."

Alex looked from Meckelson to Élie. "Come again?"

Élie looked at Alex. "Your son was with us earlier, and we were all having tea when that blonde woman from the airship came into the house."

Élie's voice suddenly sounded so far away even though he was standing right beside her.

"Where's Pierre? Is he safe? Is he hurt? Is he—"

"Miss LeBeau. Miss LeBeau. I need you to have a seat right here," she heard Meckelson say.

Alex heard Élie speaking but could not make out the words.

"Maman!"

Alex turned to her son's voice.

"Pierre!" she called back, standing.

He ran to her. "Maman, I am so glad you're here. How did you get here so fast?"

Alex looked at Meckelson, but she said nothing.

"What were you thinking, going off to Mr. Karsci and Ormont instead of home like I told you?"

"Maman."

"Don't you dare maman me! Mr. Ormont's been kidnapped, and you could've been killed."

Pierre dipped his head down. "Yes, maman."

Alex looked at Meckelson then to Élie. "Oh my gods. Did she see you? Did she hurt you?"

"No," Élie said for Pierre.

Alex cut her eyes in his direction. He stepped back.

"I saw her, but she didn't see me because Mr. Karsci had locked me in a closet. She was not looking for me. She said she wanted Rueben. Mr. Karsci said Mr. Ormont was at the den down the street. Mr. Karsci had locked me in a closet. I think she hit Mr. Karsci because when I found him, he had been knocked out. Once I was able to get him to come to, I said we needed to come here."

Alex could not stop examining her son.

"I'm all right, maman," Pierre repeated.

"Why don't you all have a seat? Officer Potkiss will take your statements in a little while," Meckelson said then took her leave.

Alex, Pierre, and Élie sat for some time.

"Who would like to start first?" the question from Officer Potkiss broke Alex out of her reverie.

"Sir," Alex began. "Our information may be tied together. Perhaps you can share about the blueprints that the blonde woman was after."

Not catching Alex's accusatory tone, Officer Potkiss made a gesture for them to follow her into a separate room.

"May I use the rest room?" Élie asked the officer. "I need to collect myself before we begin."

Alex wanted to stop him but knew it would look bizarre trying to keep him from relieving himself. Besides, they were in a police station. Élie was not getting away.

Potkiss looked a bit surprised. "Yes. I will have one of the officers escort you to the bathroom."

Officer Potkiss and Alex waited in the room.

Minutes went by, and Alex tapped her fingers on the table, waiting.

Loud shots were heard in the station lobby then close to the interrogation door. Both Potkiss and Alex ducked their heads.

"Stay down, under the desk."

Potkiss left Alex in the room and headed towards the attack in the lobby. More shots fired inside and then a whistle.

Was that a flash of color?

The smell of sulfur and more shots. She peeked from under the desk and out the glass door window.

Someone had lit fireworks inside the station.

A lot of fireworks.

After several minutes and lots of officers yelling and the snide laughter of children old enough to know better, the ruckus ceased. Alex stepped from under the table, righted herself, and left the room. The acrid smoke stung her eyes.

"I can't find him!" she heard Office Potkiss shout.

"He musta gone while these three here thought it funny to set off fireworks in the station."

Alex could not see much besides three five-foot-tall outlines being collared by an almost six-foot-tall officer.

"Élie Karsci has escaped jail!"

"You cannot escape jail if you were never arrested," Office Potkiss said.

"Well then, a possible suspect—" Potkiss held up her hand in protest. Alex continued, "A potential ally of Madam Brook-meyer's killer or possible victim has gone missing, leaving my son in danger. He's the only potential witness to the murder and kidnapping, able to describe her physical features."

Potkiss' face went from neutral to slow comprehension of the worst case scenario.

"You need to keep my son safe."

<h1 style="text-align:center">CHAPTER 11</h1>

"You will keep him in jail until you find the killer and Mister Élie," she demanded. "I need you to look after Pierre until you find out who killed Madam Brookmeyer."

"Come again," Officer Potkiss said.

"The murderer has seen my son's face, and my guess is that she knows where we and Mister Karsci live. It is not safe for my son. If you do this, you can keep it as a need to know."

"What of you and your aging mother?"

Alex stifled a laugh. Despite the birth certificate, Alex never thought her mother aged. "My mother and I are skilled enough to take care of ourselves."

"So you want us to put him back in jail?"

"Yes."

"Less than twenty-four hours after you raised Cain to get him out?"

"Yes."

"But you want us to keep him secret?"

"Yes," Alex replied.

"No."

Her face fell.

"This is not child care."

"Officer Meckelson, I am aware, but after Pierre has seen her, he is not safe staying unprotected, and neither is Mister Karsci. Assuming you find M. Karsci, I suggest you keep both in your protection until the investigation is complete or until I know my son will be safe walking about in town."

"No."

"If you say yes, I will not only provide daily meals for my son and Mister Karsci but also for you and Officer Potkiss."

Officer Meckelson stopped walking. Turned to her, "Continue."

As she explained her plan, she heard Pierre protest behind her. He did not agree that he was in danger. When he realized the plans were solid, he fell silent.

It did not occur to him that his outing with the engineers resulted in a kidnapping and the killer seeing his face.

His silence was his way of protesting.

This also would not afford her good standing in her students' eyes if they were to believe her son were a criminal.

A cloud hung over Alex's head as an officer drove her home.

"I'll only be a moment," Alex said to the officer as she let them into the house. "I'll get his clothing packed right quick."

Damn Madam Brookmeyer for getting killed, and damn my sister for coming to Honfleur, she thought as she threw several articles of clothing for Pierre for several days into a rolling satchel.

Once outside, she handed the bag to the officer, sent her on her way, and went back into the house.

Her mother was not awake but had left a note on a covered plate on the dry sink for her. Alex ate the meal in silence, washed and dried her plate, but despite the feeling of exhaustion was not tired.

Checking the ice-box and pantry for ingredients, she spotted black cocoa powder instead of traditional Dutch processed. In less than ninety minutes, she baked two dozen Black and White cookies and took a bite of one as it cooled. It had a sharpness to it with an undercurrent of sweetness. It matched her current mood.

Only four cookies were missing on the cooling rack as she retired to bed for what was left of the evening.

CHAPTER 12

Early the next morning, Alex awoke while darkness curtained the town.

The night before, Eva's note had been burning a hole in her pocket. She had read it but chose not to leave it anywhere in her room for fear it would be found. Alex memorized its message and destroyed the note. Her strides led her to the local train yard away from town.

The lamplights were sparse, and the paved roads had ended a mile back.

Must everything be so dramatic?

"Cookie!" called out a voice from the darkness. "Oh my gastronomic genius of a sister, do not tell me that you have grown tired of my pet name?"

Alex gave a deep, exaggerated sigh. "For you, I shall endure it," she replied as Eva Merchant, Ring Mistress of the Wicked Night Carnivale, stepped out of the shadows.

Eva's boots crunched against the rocks as she ran up to give Alex the tightest bear hug. Eva was the youngest of the triplets by a few minutes but had grown the tallest.

"I have missed you," she whispered against Alex. Alex embraced her sister in return before straightening.

"I need your help with finding out who is after the Committee," Alex bluntly said. "I thought it had to do with the Madam Brookmeyer blueprints, but I'm certain it involves the Committee."

Eva stood tall, tilted her chin down, and looked up at Alex. The Ring Mistress was awake at an ungodly hour at the train yard. Alex was not sure if it was done to make time to see her or for another job. Alex knew better not to ask.

"So you are looking to save the Committee?"

"Yes."

"The very Committee that is taking your son's much earned technology license away?"

"Yes," Alex hissed through her teeth.

"You and Octavia are just alike. Going out of your way to save a bunch of hypocritical citizens whose have lost their ideals and replaced them with a polite form of megalomania."

She had anticipated this from Eva and rode the wave of discontent. While Alex was like Octavia in many ways, Eva was just like their mother. When coming to either of them and asking for help, Alex had learned that unless you were absolutely certain with a choice made, either of them would question you until you broke. If you faltered, wavered for even a split moment, Eva and their mother would devour you and leave you to question your very life choices.

"Eva, this decision was not flippant."

"I cannot tell. You left us because you said, and I quote—"

Oh goodness, here we go, Alex thought.

"There needs to be a balance of power, but not at risking the equality of others."

"You are trying to force a coup d'état," Alex hissed. "That sort of thing makes a person nervous."

Eva stepped closer to Alex. "We are not trying to cause

permanent chaos but keep the equality. And not by taxing the hell out of one group. You do not have true equality if it means oppressing another group," she shot back.

"Are you going to help me or not?"

"Yes," Eva replied, "but I promise you that I will hate every moment."

"That is fine."

"Cookie, you owe me a big favor for doing this, are we clear?"

"Yes."

Such a favor came with a price. She trusted Eva and knew that when called, Eva would not put her in harm's way per se, but Alex was apprehensive as to what would be asked of her when the day came to call in that favor.

"So what did you have in mind?" Eva quietly asked. Her anger had dissolved as quickly as it arose.

"Same as always, sister," she replied. "To save the world."

"Be heroes."

"Or..." Alex thought for a moment. "Sheroes." Her sister gave her a smile and gave a slight nod in agreement.

"Cookie, I am guessing you came to me with a plan already in mind, yes?"

Alex convinced herself that she was in turn helping the police department by finding the killer and getting Rueben back to safety. She omitted the part in her mind that required her to break the laws in order to save the day.

"I would never waste your time."

"Good."

"Are Hunter and Lan still around?"

Eva stilled then slowly turned to look at Alex. "You are not messing around with this plan, are you, Cookie?"

"Not in the least."

For the first time, Eva looked a little less in control. "Are you sure you are trying to help the Committee?"

"I never said I wanted to help them. I am looking to save lives...that just happen to be on the Committee. There is a difference."

"Scared a' you, Cookie," Eva said, a smile playing at the corner of her mouth. "Scared a' you."

Alex let the warm praise wash over her. She would fix it but not alone.

L ater when Alex arrived at the cookery, things became more peculiar.

"Not a word," Guillaume finished.

"A word about what?" Alex asked.

Guillaume looked embarrassed. He was never embarrassed unless being given praise.

The students refused to look at her but looked at Guillaume for guidance.

"The students are not allowed to speak about the whereabouts of another student," he finally explained.

"Since when?"

"It's in the school handbook," Ren replied.

"Since when?" Alex asked again.

Davian glanced at the wall clock. "Ten minutes ago."

Alex side-eyed Guillaume, but he kept silent. She could not deter any of them.

"I hope you understand the ramifications of what you've chosen, I warn you."

"Warned of what? Nothing is going on here." Mr. Jones strolled past her.

"Did you hear about what happened in Savory?" Ren whispered to Baxton sitting beside her.

Baxton did not look up from his paper. "No."

"Someone found their knives in a bin."

Baxton shrugged.

"They were in a solid block of ice. Somebody must have put them in water yesterday night when they were left out and froze them."

Alex grimaced at what she overheard. It would explain the mandatory class reminder made earlier that students should "always keep your knives with you at all times."

Mr. Jones did not turn to look at Ren or Baxton seated behind him, but they knew he was addressing them. "Someone used temporary glue to adhere pencils to the desks earlier this morning, which is why everything is running behind schedule today."

Alex just shook her head. The most any of her peers had done was soak a chef's coat in water then place it in the freezer overnight, like had happened her first day at the École.

"Oh and someone hid all first-semester students' left gardening shoes too," Ren added. "It took them two hours to find them."

"Where were they?" Davian asked.

"On the shed roof."

A high-pitched scream came from the water closet down the hall.

Alex looked up, instructed her students to stay put, and went to investigate the commotion.

A student stepped out of the bathroom, red-faced, hands away from their side and their trousers soaking.

The students from other classes had stepped out of their rooms to witness the uproar.

Before Alex could open her mouth to ask, the wet student growled, "Some dunderhead thought it funny to place thick glass in between the seat and the commode!"

Davian laughed.

Alex turned to see her students not following directions.

Davian laughed long and hard.

"That is it!" the student said and walked to Mister G's office.

Alex gave her students a ten-minute break and went to Guillaume's office after the student had been consoled, given a change of clothes, and informed that the issue of pranks would be immediately addressed at the school.

"Ellec," Guillaume said in exasperation. "What am I going to do with these students? Do they not take anything sacred?"

Alex grimaced. "Guillaume, I don't think going to the bathroom..."

He waved a hand. "No, no. Not that. Last week, Chef York tells me the raw eggs he had for his students to use during stock making were boiled."

Alex stood and listened.

"You cannot make an egg raft to draw out impurities with a hardboiled egg! Ellec, if only a few eggs had been hard-boiled, I would not say a word, but four dozen eggs?" he exclaimed.

Alex's eyes bulged.

"Do you know how many deviled eggs I and the other students have had to eat last week alone?"

Alex shrugged, sure it was more than desired.

"The Misses has banned our dog from the house because I told her that he was the reason for the putrid smell assaulting our nostrils at night while we slept. I didn't have the nerve to tell her it was me and not the dog. My stomach cannot handle those eggs, and neither can my marriage."

Despite feeling awful, she laughed at her friend's delivery of the misery the school prank had caused.

"I understand, though from the looks of it, this was not done out of malice. You know how we were when we worked at... What was that restaurant where we were stagiaires?"

"La Bouche."

Alex chuckled. "That place was awful. The only way we

could face each day was the practical jokes we pulled on one another in the kitchen."

"Yes, but Ellec, this...this has gone too far. It wastes what limited supplies we have."

Alex sobered. "You are right. I will make sure to point that out to my students during our next lesson."

Later, while her students were reading and correcting their old test papers, Guillaume came running into the room.

"Good news!" Guillaume said, slightly out of breath. "They found the student's finger. It was on the floor by the entry way and not in the potato salad as previously feared."

Guillaume was struggling a bit to catch his breath.

Alex kept her face neutral in front of her class.

"Thank you, Mister G." She turned to her class. "Okay, that ends our session for today. Make sure to study for tomorrow's skills session. You are dismissed for lunch."

Without turning to the ruckus of her students vying for her attention, she left the classroom with Guillaume, hurried to his office, and closed the door.

Guillaume let out a sigh. "There is no doubt you will have their attention for the Knife Skills session."

They may not have been the ones pulling all the big pranks, but a little one couldn't hurt.

They both laughed.

CHAPTER 13

Across town, an oversized, flower-plumed hat attached to Pierre's aunt Octavia walked into the jailing area. "Pierre, come quick!"

Pierre stopped chatting with one of the prisoners. "Oh, hello Auntie Oct—"

Octavia yanked Pierre by the hand. "Ma'am," she called to the jailer. "Is there a back door?"

The jailer looked at Octavia in all her bloom as if she had gone mad.

"I take that as a no," Octavia sniffed.

Pierre allowed himself to be pulled in a circle and led to the front of the jailing area. The faint scent of his auntie's honeysuckle perfume swirled around him.

"Get down!" Octavia hissed as she shoved his head and body down behind one of the large counters.

What was going on?

He popped his head up to see. Octavia pushed him down and gave him a slight kick in the arm with the side of her skirt-covered boot.

"Guardian Reid, what a pleasant surprise," she cheerily said. Too cheery.

"Miss Laiton, I did not expect to see you here. Did you not state you had more papers to go through for the Huntingdale case?"

Aunt Octavia used her left foot to push at Pierre. Pierre sat in the spot. He watched his auntie slowly rotate her body to the right then saw the sole of her right shoe come into contact with his face.

"Oof."

"What was that, Miss Laiton? I did not catch that."

"Ah. Oof. I was going through the papers and wanted to gather more information, so I decided to talk to the authorities."

Pierre pulled away from his aunt's foot. She extended her left leg back, rotating in a circle as if searching. At that moment, Pierre understood she wanted him to move down and away from behind the counter. Still facing her, still crouched, he took steps backwards. Halfway from her, he saw Guardian Reid's shoulder as she waited for his aunt to answer her question.

Pierre's eyes watered as he kept his gaze on Reid's form and backed away. He lost sight of her as he stepped to the end of the counter just as he saw Reid face Aunt Octavia head on. If Pierre had waited any longer, Reid surely would have spotted him.

He glanced to his left, noting the pair of dark blue trousers beside him—or was it him beside it? He tilted his gaze up to the owner of the uniform.

Officer Dunbridal. Officer Potkiss' relief.

Dunbridal received the chocolates Potkiss or Meckelson did not prefer from the care packages his maman would send to the station.

Officer Dunbridal turned her palm towards Pierre as if to say wait.

"Miss Laiton," Dunbridal said then stepped opposite of Pierre and walked to the two ladies on the opposite end of the counter. "I found the papers you were looking for, but there does not seem to be any more details on what you need. You and Guardian Reid are swamped with cases, yes?"

Clearly, Officer Dunbridal was not about to reveal Pierre's situation and lose out on free chocolates.

Aunt Octavia stumbled over her words.

"Here. Why don't we ask the jailer?" Dunbridal offered. "No need to waste your time being here when you and Reid can be outside with your other charges, yes?"

"Yes," Aunt Octavia said brightly.

Officer Dunbridal stepped away from Pierre, and then three sets of footfalls drifted towards the jail area.

Tentatively, Pierre popped his head out and saw no one standing in the area where Aunt Octavia and Guardian Reid had been.

Pierre stood and looked for a place to hide.

Several of the officers at the front desk waved Pierre to them and then hid him behind it.

After what felt like forever of smelling dirt and looking at pollen-covered shoes, Pierre heard Guardian Reid's voice.

"I was told Mister LeBeau was in jail."

"Now why would he be here?" Pierre heard Dunbridal ask.

"I did not see him at the cooking school where his mother teaches," Guardian Reid said.

"I hear that sometimes if the school runs out of an item or two, they give a couple of coins to the students to purchase it at the market. I am certain that was the case."

"Was there something of concern you needed Mister LeBeau for, anything we need to get involved in?" Dunbridal asked.

"No, no. I just wanted to make sure he had not broken the licensing agreement which states arrest and the like," Reid replied. "Nevertheless, you officers have a good day."

The officer tapped Pierre's shoulder, and he stood up. His aunt was watching, he assumed, the exiting Guardian Reid. His aunt turned around and yelped at seeing Pierre.

"Goodness. I wondered where you had gone to; let us not have to do this ever again, shall we?" she said, offering her hand to him as if he were a five year old. "Now, let's get you back into jail before something bad happens."

CHAPTER 14

After lunch at the cookery, as Guillaume had predicted, Alex had the students' full attention.

"A dull knife is as dangerous as the fool yielding it," Alex began. "You will most likely be using a paring knife more often than a large chef's knife due to the nature of our position as pastry chefs, but it is best to understand all the tools in the tool box for future reference."

She waited for the last student to jot down their note before speaking.

"When you pick up and test the weight of the knives as if you were Goldilocks and the Three Bears, trying to find the right fit? Most certainly you are testing the bolster of the knife." Alex pointed to the steel between the blade and handle. "I test mine by letting it lie across my middle and index finger like so."

Raising her blade slightly, she demonstrated for the students. It took effort for Alex not to burst into giggles when mentioning the tang of the knife. "As you see, the handle, known as the pommel, should not be too heavy. If so, it will not only become a chore for you to cut items. But also if too light, you run into other issues. It must be just right for you. Not every knife is a perfect fit for every hand."

The students began testing the weight of their own school-issued chef's knives.

"You may have in your mind the kind of blade you want, and it could be the top of the line, but if it doesn't have the right weight or the handle does not grip right, step away. Your comfort is first and foremost of importance. You may never use knives often in your career as a pastry chef. But when you are cooking at home, you still want to make sure you have the right equipment for you. Take care of the second most important tool for a chef."

A hand shot up in the air.

"Yes?"

"Chef," Davian began. "What is the first?"

Alex smiled. "Pastry bag with proper tip. So," she continued, "if you do not have access to a mortar and pestle, you may use the butt of your knife to crush or bruise garlic or herbs. Oh, if you only remember one thing from today, it is this: If you drop your knife, do not, I repeat, do not try to catch it from falling on the floor."

Most of the students nodded sagely in agreement.

Once she went through the basics, she brought them into the kitchen to practice hands-on. She circled each student's station, watching.

"Mr. Jones," Alex said, placing a hand on his shoulder. She looked at his face, attempting to catch his eye, but he looked just past her for a moment before turning his attention back to the cutting board.

"May I?" she asked, her hands hovering over his. Alex guided his hand in a rocking motion. "Do you feel that movement? That is what you want; find the rhythm. There's a count to it, no?"

She took her hand away and watched Mr. Jones mimic her movement, his technique corrected.

"Each item you chop or slice has a rhythm. Your job is to find it."

"Just like music."

Alex blinked in surprise. A simple waltz count came to mind. "Yes," she said in surprise. "Just like music."

Mr. Jones did not split his focus as he continued to work on his rhythm until lunch break.

Ren offered to assist Alex in setting up for the next baking demonstration where the students would practice their paring skills.

"To maintain order in a kitchen, you need to know the rules," Alex began when her students were seated.

Davian raised his hand. "But Chef Heston told us to break the rules in the kitchen."

Alex paused before replying. "With the desserts you make, not in the job title you hold in the kitchen. I have noted there is no rotation for brigade jobs here, and I will guess you all have chosen what you like to do the most and stick whoever lost a bet with the dishes. Correct?"

The students all looked at their feet.

"From now on, everyone washes dishes, everyone does their assigned job, and no one is self-appointed *sous chef* in this class without my permission."

They all just stared dumbly at her.

"Class? Who can tell me which brigade position is the most important one?"

"The chef de cuisine or executive chef," Mr. Jones replied. "She can do all the jobs in the kitchen but not the other way around."

Alex nodded. "Good point. Except although she may be able to make a meal or two alone, she cannot run a restaurant kitchen and provide meals for the patrons by herself. *Every* job is of importance. If one of your team falls behind, it affects everyone in the kitchen, from the dishwasher to the saucier."

Mr. Jones looked surprised at being corrected.

"Omit the dishwasher from a restaurant kitchen, and tell me their role is of less importance."

Understanding crossed Mr. Jones' face.

"Now," Alex began. "Let us go through the jobs you will take on. Knowing this will help you when you are a commis at the school restaurant. Now, who can tell me the difference between a *pâtissier,* a *boulanger,* and a *glacier?* And what role does a pâtissier play if there is no boulanger in the kitchen?"

Teaching went as smoothly as it could despite the entire class discovering the lack of towels in the room. In fact, every towel on the floor was missing, which was to everyone's chagrin when two hapless students grabbed the tong handles.

Both Baxton and Alex dashed out of the room to find Davian and Ren holding the tongs with one hand while looking at their other hands with horror. Alex crossed the room and examined the sticky concoction on the tongs handle.

"Honey," she said, "nothing to fret over. Go find out how many of the utensils are covered, and then go wash them and your hands."

"Yes, chef," they said feebly before shuffling off.

"Today, you have a choice between making a Crostata di Frutta or Ricotta. If you choose fruit, your choices of jam are apricot, brambleberry, or peach. If you choose to make it with sweetened ricotta, you can use either anisette, anise," she translated, "or with chocolate. Please note that if I catch you drinking the anisette, you will be expelled immediately from school. Do I make myself clear?"

All the students nodded.

"Now, if you would like to try your hand at making it with

pastry cream, also known as crema paticerra, know that the ingredients are waiting for you in the walk-in refrigerator."

Despite it being humid and summer, Alex, being a chocolatier, decided to demonstrate the crostata di ricotta. She decided to blind-bake the crostata as she put ground hazelnut into the melted semisweet chocolate ganache.

After the demonstration and as her dough baked, Alex circled the room to each station, offering a tip here and there.

"You are rushing," Alex said quietly as she came to Ren's station.

"But you gotta be fast in a kitchen."

Alex nodded. "Efficient, not fast. Fast does not always bring about a clean, finished product."

Ren grimaced.

"You will be fast when you have a stronger foundation to pull from, but at this moment, you are attempting to do it all." She leaned into Ren, "You don't need to prove anything to me; just prove it to yourself."

Ren looked at her in surprise.

"From now on, I want you to read all recipes three times, not two. You are to do the same with directions. If you do not understand something or believe a step was missed, ask. Do not wing it—at least not yet. If you forget how something is put together, ask."

"But what if the chef yells at me or calls me useless because I don't know how?"

Alex looked at Ren. "Then you know two things. One, they are a *trou du cul.*"

Ren gasped then giggled.

"And two, they are not very good at their job as a leader. If a chef does not make the time for the crew, there will never be a staff that stays."

Alex patted Ren's shoulder before she checked on her cooling dessert.

Once her dessert had fully cooled, while her students were in the process of creation in different forms, Alex took the Italian pastries out and adorned them with fan-sliced strawberries.

Alex went to each student and offered a piece of pastry before dismissing them for the day.

Guillaume came through the door. "Chef, may I have a moment?"

Guillaume was oddly formal and polite. No mirth behind his eyes like when they had pulled the prank on her students earlier.

Alex's stomach dropped. The moment they were in the wine pantry, Guillaume unleashed a barrage of sentences that Alex could barely string together.

Body. Missing. Part. Found.

"Slow down. Start from the beginning."

"Chef Heston. His body was found. Well, the parts that allowed him to be identified. Murdered. They think it happened a few days before you arrived."

Her mouth dropped open. "Why would anyone do such a thing?"

Guillaume shrugged. "I do not know. He was not the nicest man, as is with some in our field, but not hated enough to kill. In the end, he was a bit rough but promised to make an effort. He even cut down his hours at the Wild Mare so he could focus."

"Wild Mare?" she said dumbly.

"Yes. It was a schedule I had to work around when I first hired him. He occasionally worked school events but only if they were events that would put his name in the papers. That's why when he went missing before the airship event I was so surprised. He left no note as to where he had gone. I checked the brothel, and they hadn't seen him either. His clients were left wondering about his whereabouts too," he said. Then, mostly to himself, "Seems I was not the only one."

"Guillaume?"

"Yes."

"Did he ever brag about any of his clients?"

"No. I would not have brought the conversation to that place anyways, respecting the women's privacy and such."

"I understand. I was just wondering if there may have been someone, maybe a client, that wasn't happy with his services anymore."

"I do not know. The Wild Mare doesn't deal in seedy clientele, and they make sure to keep their men safe. Besides, the officers said that they suspect his...his murder happened while he was not working at the brothel. A rare day off, I think. Though still, something just doesn't feel right."

Alex put her hand on his arm. "I'm sorry, Guillaume. Is there anything I can do?"

He patted her hand back. "No, Ellec. Just keep on with your lessons. The students enjoy it. I..." He trailed off. "I," he continued, "I need to make an announcement to the faculty and students."

Leaving him to collect his thoughts seemed the wisest action.

Guillaume was the only one left alone that day, and Alex was grateful her own classes had concluded.

Alex could only guess that the murders were tied together but had nary a clue as to how. She needed to clear her head.

When the students had cleared out the demo kitchen and the building was close to silent, Alex went through the pantry, grabbed supplies, and began to create.

Pâte de fruit was Alex's favorite candy to eat during her wandering chef days in parts of France. When she was eating too many of them, she convinced herself to learn to make them. She begged for lessons from the mother of the chef de cuisine of the restaurant Alex had worked in at the time.

When watching another create the confection, Alex, in her hindsight, could say the candy only seemed easy to make until it became her turn. It was deceptive. She deemed the longest hour was staring at the thermometer to maintain a precise temperature. To make things worse, the waiting was not overnight but several days for the treat to cure before dressing it up in caster sugar.

The kitchen smelled of tropical flowers Alex had once seen in a private botanical garden. As she waited for the confection to set, she warmed several containers holding different colored cocoa butter.

Once at the right temperature, she poured them in tiny bowls. Working fast, Alex painted designs inside molds before each of the colors cooled. By the end of the painstaking, quick work, she mentally praised herself for her design.

As it firmed, she set the small ration of bittersweet chocolate to temper in the double boiler.

She checked on the pâte de fruit. Only the center jiggled a bit, and the rest of the dessert had firmed. She took a clean knife and sliced an inch thick and wide piece away and made a rough chop.

With the tempered chocolate, she made a fine shell in each distinctive mold and let each rest to cool and dry without streaks.

Hours later, she had a tropical chocolate bar adorned with a beautiful lady on the front. Alex decided it her current best work.

Later at home as she finally readied for bed, she heard a tapping at her door.

"Alex," her mother said softly.

Alex crossed the room and opened the door.

"Eva needs to see you tomorrow evening."

"When?"

Maman Eloisa pursed her lips as she handed her the note. Alex looked at her mother's scrawl.

"Just...you both keep yourselves safe. You hear me," was all her mother said before leaving her alone for the evening.

CHAPTER 15

The following morning proved difficult for Alex to get out of bed, but she managed and got to the cookery with fifteen minutes to spare before the first session.

Due to the season and lack of living relatives, the wake for Madam Brookmeyer would happen later that day. Until then, Alex had a class to teach.

"I'll be demoing ice cream today. I had planned to do it during the heat wave, but perhaps it's better that I not rush through in an attempt to keep things cool, yes?"

Her students' eyes lit up.

"Cream Ice, as it had first been known," she began, "was a favorite with President George Washington. How he would spend several hundred dollars on such a confection was not understood by many unless they had been privileged to taste such a creation."

Alex could not imagine the headache of keeping such frozen without the ice-houses, steam-powered motors, and refrigeration units of the current day. Despite the resistance, she enjoyed soda sundaes made with soda, but surely she did not have enough appetite to eat the large batch she would test out.

"At first, I thought of going with tradition and making Orange Blossom because it's simple, but the familiarity of it is boring. I blame the chance meeting I had with a cone of sea-salted caramel ice cream I tasted on my first day back in Honfleur."

She instructed Ren and Davian to go to the pantry to discover what abundant ingredients the school had, ones that, if used, would not inflate the buying budget.

"If you find any cherries, know they are off limits."

"Perhaps we could use a little juice from it?" Baxton offered.

Alex thought for a moment. "If there is a bottle of amaretto around, I'm sure that would make a good combination."

"Or better would be a simple, amaretto-flavored ice cream with a spiced cherry syrup that has the consistency of pourable caramel but not too sweet," Mr. Jones offered.

Alex smiled.

"Davian, can you grab two copper pots and get them on the stove?"

Davian walked out of the room, and Alex prepared the scale on the large table for the influx of ingredients arriving.

When all the students arrived back into the demo kitchen and grabbed a stool to sit around the table, she pulled out the pencil and writing pad from her short work apron pocket and began to figure out the ratios needed.

Alex made efforts to discuss her process in creating the best recipe—the importance of knowing food chemistry and understanding how to use what was at hand.

"No matter how much you plan, the worst could happen in your kitchen, and you need to improvise. It is not only about thinking on your feet but it's understanding the properties of the ingredients you have on hand."

She put her pencil down. "The almond flavor could be achieved with an abundance of amaretto in the cream, but that would cause an issue where the frozen treat would never harden due to too much alcohol. And choosing finely crushed almond flour would promise broken teeth."

"No one would ever eat at my restaurant again if I did that," Baxton retorted.

"Yes, so pay attention."

She crossed out the measurements and tried again to find the fat-to-alcohol ratio that would allow her to replicate the rich, melting-on-her-tongue reaction—the way the other ice cream had behaved.

With the answer not coming easily, her students shouted out possible solutions and answered her barrage of "why" queries. They seemed to enjoy this part of the process more than she in recipe creation. Like solving a puzzle that you could eventually eat.

Her memory held too many recipes and ideas but nothing concrete enough for her to feel confident about her figures adding true. In true example, Alex reached for the school's textbook on food science and chemistry to gain further insight and prevent any wastefulness on her experiment. While mentally going through her numbers, she prepped the wooden ice cream barrel to cool the concoction to frozen levels.

"Okay, I think that will work," she offered. Satisfied, she measured out her ingredients.

"I got exhausted just watching you. I need a break," Davian said.

"Just for that, you get to put crushed ice in a bowl. Place an empty bowl atop of it, and then meet us at the stove."

Gathered around the iron stove, Alex kept the heat low as

to scorch, not boil, the heavy cream while keeping her eye on the second saucepan with the spiced cherry syrup ingredients.

"The base cream concoction will not take long to blend. Ren, hand me that strainer. I like to be extra careful just in case I curdled the cream," she said before pouring it through the mesh strainer into the empty bowl sitting over the ice.

"As we allow that to begin the cooling process, let us turn our sights onto the syrup. Davian, get water on that brush, and brush the inner sides of the pan to keep the beaded sugar down. Unsavory crystals do not make a delicious treat for this smooth ice cream."

Instead of relying only on her vision, she used a thermometer to test the contents. While they stood around and waited, Alex quizzed them on cook times for cooking sugar.

"That looks about right," she announced after. "Pour the spices and extract in."

Baxton did as instructed, and Alex took the pot off the eye and did a gentle swirl until all the spices were incorporated before pouring the contents into a canning jar to cool.

"Now for the boring part. Clean the dirty dishes we've made."

Everyone groaned but helped out as she glanced at the clock to realize her window for getting the base into the wooden barrel was closing.

"You'd better finish up or else we may not get this ice cream made."

For the first time, Alex did not hear them argue over who would wash or dry or put away any of the used equipment. With speed, they were gathered around the wooden bucket and attentive to not only make but sample what would be almond ice cream with spiced cherry syrup on top.

Each student either lingered on the flavors on a bare spoon or spoke amongst one another on how to make the frozen treat better or pair new flavors for something different.

Later that day, while preparing for Madam Brookmeyer's wake, Alex transferred the variety of cheeses from the local cheese monger. She placed the blue cheese chocolate truffles she'd hand-rolled onto the thin, slate tablet.

Honfleur townsfolk were out around town, enjoying the break from the heat wave, which Alex took full advantage of by choosing to bring blue cheese and other assortments to the wake.

Alex placed the slate on the table with other food items.

She was taken aback at how jovial the funeral attendants were. The wake's tone was more a soirée than a loss of a philanthropist.

A group swarmed around a blond-haired gentleman, and when someone stepped back, Alex gasped. The man's features were similar to the late Madam Brookmeyer.

"Uncanny, isn't it?" asked a voice in her ear. She looked at the man. "Dr. Featherton," he said and held out his hand.

She took it and let him do the formalities and then took back her hand.

"Her son," Dr. Featherton explained. "He's heir to a large transportation fortune."

Alex steeled her expression. The Committee would never let him inherit all that money unless he was from Indigenous or Diaspora ancestry.

"Don't you worry about the Committee. Junior there has no clue about science. He'd rather be working on enjoying the financial fruits of his now late mother's money than do any work."

Alex watched Junior take a bite of the truffle then take

another and another. He consumed the entire batch, leaving none for any of the grieving guests.

Dr. Featherton said, reading her thoughts, "He eats when he's depressed. He's depressed a lot."

She shook her head. "That's too bad, but nowadays, we have special powders, medicines, that can help curb the blues."

Dr. Featherton said nothing but nodded in agreement. "You can't give him too much grief; he just lost his meal ticket."

Alex turned to look at Dr. Featherton. Surely he was joking. Dr. Featherton's face was serious. She felt more depressed for not just the loss of a great woman but for the person that couldn't appreciate the brilliance.

She was looking at Junior's animated face when it suddenly became serious. His mouth went into a frown before he crashed to the floor.

Someone stepped in and went to the young, unconscious man. Alex assumed she was a doctor and one who was Junior's because she seemed to be familiar with him and wouldn't answer questions of the guests. The doctor checked Junior's pulse then after a few minutes shook his head.

The doctor roughly rolled Junior on his side.

"What was he eating before he lost consciousness?" she asked the guests surrounding her.

They all looked stunned and unable to find the words. "Those chocolate truffles," said one finally. "All of them. I think there were thirty of them too. I got one before he ate the rest. They were good."

Everyone's eyes bulged. The doctor lost composure then asked, "Who made them?"

Alex's stomach dropped. "I did. Why?"

The doctor called out to her, "What did you put in them?"

"Apples, cranberries, walnuts, and blue cheese. Oh and chocolate and cream, of course."

The doctor looked at her as if thinking. "How many pounds of blue cheese did you use?"

"Not much. Why?"

The doctor's head dropped. "Come with me," she said under her breath then took off her jacket and put it over Junior's face.

The doctor walked out of the room, and Alex followed.

"You should really put a list of ingredients on your items, you know that?" the doctor shouted at her.

Alex stepped back. "There was nothing in there that could harm," she shot back.

The doctor looked frustrated and spat out, "It is if your client is taking medicine that is contra-indicated."

Alex looked confused.

"It's an anti-depressant, and it does not mix well with blue cheese."

Alex's hand shot up to her mouth. "Oh my—"

Alex LeBeau had accidently killed Madam Brookmeyer's heir.

Plates crashed to the floor. Someone had tripped over Junior's body and fallen.

Junior coughed out a blue cheese chocolate truffle—or what was left of it—and took several gasping breathes of air.

"Is this a two-for-one, Chef?" Officer Meckelson asked as Alex was escorted into the station.

Alex stayed silent but wondered if Meckelson ever went home. She also hoped she was not placed in or near the same cell as her son. Alex was beginning to think she had bad mojo. If things got any worse, she would have to carry a gris-gris bag with her.

"You may go."

Alex turned to the officer. "Pardon?"

Officer Meckelson walked close to Alex, leaned in, and whispered in her ear, "He's not dead. He just choked on one of your truffles, and the nearness of death caused him to confess his and Mr. Featherton's intentions. Dr. Featherton has been all over the country using long-lost sons and daughters to claim a fortune that is not theirs to receive. There will be more coming out of the woodwork."

Alex dumbly stared at the officer.

The officer looked back at her. "You did not find any of this suspicious? Your truffles are not only good but they're not deadly."

Alex searched for words. "Thank you?"

The officer shrugged.

"Maman," Pierre hissed. "Come here. I have news."

CHAPTER 16

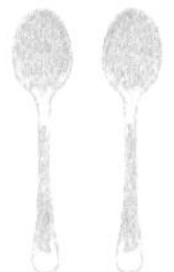

Alex stepped to him and dipped her head to hear him as he whispered.

"That crazy man," Pierre began. "The one you fought during the fireworks."

Alex nodded.

"He was making such a ruckus and causing all sorts of trouble last night, even after some of the students came by to drop off some dinner for me and the officers. They offered him some, and it set him off. They had to be escorted out. We were all scared. It got so bad that the officers had to take him to another station because they said they didn't have a safe enough cell to keep him from harming himself."

Alex waited patiently for her son to get to the point.

"He said something about that blonde lady."

Alex perked up. "Which blonde lady?"

"The one you called Furious Angel, but he didn't call her that. He was screaming about how he was like a brother to his...Boss Lady. He said if he was harmed, his Boss Lady would exact revenge on them the way she did when her brother Tabbis died."

Alex looked at Pierre, her eyes widened.

"He then started screaming some gibberish then said, 'Maggie is gonna kill you!' Well, not you, but the officers taking him away."

"Yes, I figured," Alex said.

"So, I don't know if you can do anything with that information, but it seemed really important."

"You are right. It is."

"I guess it was a good thing I'm in jail."

Alex winced. Pierre must have seen her face.

"Sorry. I meant to say—"

Alex held up a hand. "I know what you meant. I will look into it further. Until then, you get some rest. I'll be back soon."

During her break, instead of staying in the kitchen to prep for the next day, Alex did not take comfort in knowing the path to the police station better than her town's library. Once justice had been claimed and Pierre was safe, Alex promised to never put herself into situations again that would require police intervention.

She wasn't sure what she was looking for but knew if she asked a librarian for assistance in the search, she would be far better off. Librarians made the best researchers.

"I need to look up information on stillbirths."

"Excuse me?" The librarian looked at her. "Ma'am, are you looking for medical facts or newspaper mentions?"

"Of one child. I have a name. Tabbis."

Alex did not want to search for any such thing, but it seemed the only lead that may give a clue to where Rueben was being kept. Much to her horror, she sifted through newspaper clippings and pictures she would never be able to scrub from her memory. To make it worse, she found no mention of a child with that name.

"There's no child, but there is a mention of a young man with the last name of Tabbis that passed away year ago and is," the librarian stopped, held the newspaper closer as he looked over his glasses, "survived by his only living relative, Margaret Tabbis, a clerk for the Committee."

Alex leaned over and looked at the clipping. From the obituary, Maggie Tabbis' brother had been just a decade older than Pierre.

"Odd," the librarian said. "There's no mention of his first name. It just says A. Tabbis. Maybe they were embarrassed."

CHAPTER 17

Alex tried to be simple and cohesive with her thoughts so as not to confuse him. She could not receive help if she was not able to ask for it in a skilled way.

"You are looking for any articles on Madam Brookmeyer, yes?"

The librarian brought her to the card catalog, and she put him to work in search of every article about Madam Brookmeyer, but they were few and far between. Very little had been written about the woman, but much had been discussed about her husband.

How curious that so much would be written about a man in the paper in this day and age. He must have been an extraordinary man to be acknowledged in the papers.

"Since there is so little about Madam, perhaps we should look for her husband's name as the primary mention?"

The librarian looked taken aback. "A man in the paper in regards to scientific advancement? That will be rare and probably easier to find."

He was not wrong. In this day and age, advancements in

technology were female-driven, especially with the restrictions put on males. Not much was being seen by men or celebrated from what Alex had observed.

Their world seemed to have shifted, swinging heavily the other way since the Insurrection. Alex could not fathom a world in which the Indigenous, women, and people of color were treated as anything but equals. How horrible the world would be if the country had gone to war over such injustices. They were equal. No war needed to drive home such a truth.

The Insurrection had a body count, but the participants tried to keep the numbers low in an attempt to keep things from escalating into a war in which friends, lovers, and families would be divided. During the few times in her life when she found herself thinking about a history she was never a part of, she wondered if people, some people, men, had wished for things to stay the same.

It was not a question or discussion one had in good company, so she stayed silent with others, but raising an Anglo-looking male made her hyper-aware of who had become the minority of their world.

One could only look at the United Kingdom's need to colonize India, Vietnam, and other places to see why the Committee was formed in the first place.

How America was founded was a stain in the history books for all time. It was not something many wanted to repeat or have hanging over their heads. Alex was in a unique position, in which as a woman of color, she had an easy time of navigating through this world. Granted, she was not given things and did have to work and train for all that she enjoyed.

Her son, on the other hand, though mixed, had the unfortunate luck of lacking any melanin. He was always her beloved son, but her love could not protect him from the oddities of this world. Though her son was one, to gaze at him reminded many older ones of a past she could not comprehend. In that past, oppression, slavery, and other forms of violence were a societal foundation, a checklist of daily living.

Sure, she could have come at each person that stared suspiciously at her boy and spoken the defensive words, "Not all white men!" but it distracted from the bigger picture.

The past, as horrible as it had been, was real and served as a warning to everyone not to repeat history. The past reminded Alex that her blackness was not a shield for Pierre, nor did her son expect it.

She reminded herself that her son's whiteness was not what made her son a victim. The fact that he had been accused of something he did not commit was the focus. The only person whose opinion could destroy Pierre's career chances had let prejudice get in her way.

Whatever the reasoning behind Guardian Reid's bias, Alex did not care to know it. She was not the woman's psychiatrist nor closest confidant to find out such origins of ideas.

Pierre's freedom and licensing were at stake. Alex was no fool. The world did not play fair, but it did not mean all was lost. She would use her privilege for good only because she had the ability.

While she agreed with the ideals the Committee stood for, at least during their conception, Alex could only admit to herself that she saw things shifting for them and not in a positive way.

She had overheard rumors that the Committee was headed for a fall and the question of "Why would anyone want to not have equal rights?"

No one seemed to ask the real question. How long would pissed off white men take it before they flipped the script?

The Furious Angel was not male and pale, but perhaps she had seen the other side of things. Surely nothing ever could compare to slavery and genocide, but to some misguided souls, their threatened emotional comfort was a direct correlation.

Alex stopped glancing over the newspapers.

"Sir? Can we look up when Madam Brookmeyer first began working with the engineers?"

"Oh, yes."

The first newspapers the librarian found to mention the collaboration between the engineers and Madam Brookmeyer was from late the previous year. Alex had still been living in New Virginia.

With fingertips gliding over the text, Alex kept her finger on the obituary section of another paper. Madam Brookmeyer had started collaborating only months after her husband's passing.

Alex sat back in her chair, mulling the information about in her head.

The Furious Angel was tied to all of this somehow, and revenge was arguably the motivation.

Why kill someone that does not seem to be connected to you in any way or form? Then perhaps thievery was the motivation.

Maybe the Furious Angel had their work stolen. The only logical reason why she would be looking for blueprints after killing Brookmeyer. To take back what was hers and do so as a punishment, a warning perhaps for any other thieves in the industry.

One hell of an elaborate murder plan.

Alex glanced at the clock on the wall. If she did not leave, she would be late with her rendezvous with Eva. She thanked the librarian for his assistance and left.

Why not just steal back the blueprints just as the Furious Angel had done that night at Brookmeyer's home? Alex thought as she headed out to meet Eva.

"Sister," Eva hissed. "Come, before we are spotted."

Alex hitched herself onto the horse her sister provided and followed her out of town.

An hour later, in the middle of packed trees surrounding the hangar, she dismounted her horse.

"This is the worst idea I've ever had."

"Cookie, it was my idea!" Eva replied as she hid the horses from sight.

Alex followed behind Eva. "Exactly."

"That does not make sense."

Alex hissed, "Neither does my agreeing to be here."

She waved her arms in the general area of the empty Damask Hangar.

Nudging Alex out of the way, Eva tentatively stepped forward, tapping her intricately black-lace-adorned, leather booted on the ground. Pebbles and stones scraped against the ground; then, there was a hollow thud. Eva's foot found the groove on the hatchway.

After Brookmeyer's machine was stolen from the Damask Hangar, access had been closed off, but Eva found a way in.

Both women got to their knees and looked for the handle. A small patch of leather covered the keyhole. Alex pushed Eva aside by the shoulder, took a hairpin from her hair, and stuck it in the lock. She had accidently left her lock picking set back at Maman Eloisa's house.

Within moments, it bent beyond use.

She pulled out another one and, with less enthusiasm, worked the lock for several minutes before it sprang open.

Alex and Eva looked at one another and smiled before opening the hatchway.

"Is anyone going to find us here?"

Eva shook her head. "It's been blocked off."

"What's here? The police could not have missed anything...could they?"

Eva looked at her sister, her eyes bright.

"I think this is where she set up things way before the airship situation."

Alex did not need to ask Eva who she meant.

Eva gently closed the hatch behind her, and Alex waited for her eyes to adjust to the pitch black.

As her eyes adjusted, Alex stepped slowly, putting a foot out for the last step only to find that there wasn't one. Her straight leg jammed into her hip. Sparks shot up her leg. She muffled a gasp.

"You all right?" Eva whispered.

"Yes," Alex replied through her teeth.

When her eyes adjusted, Alex spotted heavy curtain against a transom window. She pulled back the tiny curtain to let in the natural mid-afternoon light and with it a scene that was unnatural.

A dummy stood before Alex and Eva wearing a leather bodysuit but with spikes all over it, resembling a porcupine. Eva walked over to examine it. Alex's focus followed down to the tube attached to a ball that traveled the length of the arm. Each spike was hollowed out just enough to pierce the skin and thick enough to carry something within the needles.

This was a weapon. A suit shaped like a man that could extract a toxic revenge. The needles were three inches in length. One of the suits looked like it had been covered in dirt. Clumps of mud stuck to the front. A crushed red berry peeked from underneath the foot of the dummy's boot. Alex stopped walking along the path row made of suits.

What was in the needles?

Behind the porcupine of destruction was a large cover, like a curtain but lighter fabric. Her stomach turned, and her pulse quickened. Alex's fingers traced the fabric before giving it a huge tug.

"What is it?" Alex turned to her well-traveled sister.

Eva shook her head. An errant strand from her coiffed hair fell near her cheek. "I have never seen such a thing before."

"An airship that vertically lifts with those blades."

Alex walked towards it, craning her neck.

"You see that hose? I think it's what powers it."

Alex hunched down, looking for the end of the tube. "There you are!"

Eva ran to her, ready to fight. "There is nothing there but a boiler."

"You know, Eva, even when we were children, you never did respect the brilliance of invention."

"Cookie, what is it that you are looking at? I do not see anything but aluminum blades attached to a boiler," Eva spat back.

Alex circled the skeletal structure, ignoring the way her always-composed sister lost her composure. "Question is not what it is but how did they get it in this space because it certainly was not by that tiny hatch."

Eva stopped midsentence. "That's right."

Footsteps came from the wall behind the metal blade piece.

"Come," Eva said and attempted to throw the drape back over the piece. Alex quickly assisted, keeping an ear out for the footsteps echoing louder.

Once done, Eva grabbed Alex by the arm and pulled her up the stairs and through the hatch. Putting everything where she found it, Alex helped her sister erase their footprints to and from the door then high-tailed it into the trees.

By the time they reached the horses, they were breathing heavily. Alex hoisted herself on the back horse and followed her sister towards town.

What now? What did she do with this information? What was it that she and her sister discovered?

Furious Angel was not just a murderer. She was capable of engineering something that was brilliant, but Alex would bet dollars to doughnuts it would not be used for good.

Alex grimaced.

Nothing was scarier than a bitter engineer.

Though one nagging question kept pushing at her, why kidnap the engineer if she already had the blueprints?

If the Furious Angel was out for revenge, why not kill the engineers Brookmeyer had hired in the Furious Angel's place?

There had been no paper trail against Brookmeyer for the newest innovation, which Alex was still not clear on since the big reveal did not happen due to Brookmeyer's surprising demise.

The engineers did not speak of it either, but was it out of loyalty to Brookmeyer? Or a need for the engineers to take said plans and find another deep pocket investor?

Without looking at her sister, she knew Eva would tell her to follow the money. Though with both Brookmeyers dead and no known living relatives, any money left would probably be given to charities of some sort. That was common for rich types like Madam Brookmeyer.

But the killing by Rueben's contraption smelled of personal motivation, not monetary.

If killing for personal gain, the job would be done and the murderer would go on their way, but Furious Angel stayed to watch. Furious Angel had donned a persona, interacted with Brookmeyer for several hours, watched the murder happen, and then leapt out of the ship. Alex had to hand it to her—Furious Angel was quite thorough and detail-oriented in executing a plan.

"I know who did it. I think I know who killed Madam Brookmeyer."

Eva had slowed their pace as they reached Honfleur town green.

"What is that, Cookie?"

"Furious Angel was at the party the entire time, but Brookmeyer did not recognize her. That would mean either Furious Angel had been in disguise or Brookmeyer did not know Furious Angel from Eve, as the saying goes."

Eva grew quiet. Both of them in their thoughts.

Alex mentally backtracked in her memory of all she could remember of the guests. Outside the kitchen, her memory was shaky, though anything revolving around the food gave her clear recall.

"The introduction of guests and Madam Brookmeyer had not thought of where Furious Angel sat or who she had pretended to be. There was the high-named guest who had been cleared and their security personnel," Alex stated as they sauntered into town. "Both sets knew one another," she continued. "Brookmeyer knew them, but it was not enough that those guests were surprised and in shock for her murder."

"I would advise interviewing them, but who has the time?

Between trying to keep Pierre safe, our sister Octavia's misguided efforts to help, and teaching for Guillaume, you do not have the time let alone the attention span."

Alex nodded then looked at the time on her wrist. If she did not get back to the school, her students would not be given their newest assignment.

"Speaking of such sister, I must head off. May I drop off the horses with you?"

"We can ride to the school beforehand," Eva offered.

"No, no. I need to go to the station to talk with Pierre. There's something I am missing, but I cannot put my finger on it. He was there, and maybe he can help me figure that out."

"Fair. Cookie, keep yourself safe. If you need any more help, you know where to find me."

Alex gave her sister a nod and dismounted.

"Eva?"

The statuesque beauty turned.

"At the library, I may have figured out her name, but I'm not sure. It said she worked for the Committee."

Eva's eyebrows lifted, showing curiosity.

"Maybe I should go to Octavia about it?"

"Why?"

"The obituary said that an A. Tabbis was survived by his sister Margaret Tabbis. I figured since Octavia works for the Committee, she could do a little recon for me."

Eva slowly shook her head. "Cookie, I'll handle it."

Alex squinted. "But Octavia could actually—"

"Alex, she's one of ours. Maggie Tabbis is one of our agents."

It was settled, and Alex dropped the subject and left her sister's company. On her way back to the cookery, Alex realized she would need to wash up and remove any debris from her hair in order to keep from drawing suspicion.

CHAPTER 19

In the school, before Alex could right herself, Guillaume pulled her away from the students and into a room offset from the main classes.

"Guillaume, why are we standing in the wine pantry and not taking a bottle of wine?" Alex asked, swatting a fruit fly away from her face.

"Because I need to think, and this is the only place I can go for some peace."

At that moment, the door opened. One of the students popped their head in. "Mister G, are you down there?"

Alex suppressed a giggle.

"I will be up in fifteen minutes. I just need fifteen minutes," he hissed and threw his hat at the door.

It slammed shut, and Alex put her hand over her mouth to keep from laughing out loud. He went to where his hat landed and picked it up, crumpling it in his nervous grip.

Guillaume sighed.

"Alex, I will miss this the most when the school is no more."

Alex stopped laughing. "No. We will get through this; you will see."

He tilted his head up towards the wooden ceiling. "I worked so hard to bring this school to life. What am I to tell the instructors? What do I tell the students?"

Alex sensed that he was not asking her but looking for guidance from someone that was no longer in the land of the living. She waited patiently for him to conclude his silent thoughts.

"My friend, the rumors have already begun."

"Begun for what? You did not murder Madam Brookmeyer, and neither did the food."

"I know that," he spat then pointed to her. "And you know that, but that is not what people read in the paper."

No matter how unfair or untrue, gossip spread faster than praise. If only the happy people wrote reviews in abundance instead of the angry, bitter, or gossip mongering ones.

"There have been three cancellations for the Autumn semester. I am certain those are not the last."

Alex stayed quiet. He was not asking her to fix a thing, and frankly, she had no solution. She could only listen.

"Brookmeyer was to be what got the school attention, but this was not what we ever expected."

Whoever said bad attention was still attention was not in the culinary field.

"How is the student restaurant doing financially?"

Guillaume shrugged. "Not so bad, but if another story about Brookmeyer dying while dining on the students' food goes out again, I do not think those numbers will be so strong."

Alex nodded in agreement.

"I cannot stop the newspaper from printing what they print, and I will not write a letter to them. That is as bad as writing a rebuttal to a bad review of your restaurant. You may feel grand writing it, but once it is public, you are raked over the coals. I saw such a thing happen with Chef Xavier. Never did recover."

Alex stood in silence. Everyone knew Chef Xavier's story. He had become the parable told to new chefs in terms of how not to behave when on the receiving end of a biting review. Rumor was Chef Xavier was now busboy Xavier, but she could not confirm it.

He turned from her and let a string of curses fly. Guillaume never thought it polite to curse in front of people but somehow had convinced himself that if you could not see his face, he was technically not cussing in front of you.

"Guillaume," she called, but he continued. "Guillaume!"

Her yelling jolted him out of his colorful, foul-mouth monologue.

He turned to her.

"You have five minutes to wallow, and then you go do something else. Okay?"

He closed his mouth and nodded at her in agreement. "You are right."

"Now, many more things will come your way, but you are strong and clever. You have gotten this far in life, and it is not easy for a man such as you," she gestured to the skin on his arm.

"What you are going to do," she continued, "is take this attention and spin it to suit the school."

"But how?"

Alex squeezed his arm. "Be clever," she replied.

He thought for a moment then said, "Honfleur Cooking School. Food to die for!"

Alex blinked, wide-eyed and non-committal. She did not want to shoot down his efforts right out of the gate.

"That's a start. Very...macabre," she struggled out. "Very gallows humor of you. Perhaps you can work on it more?"

The fear was gone from Guillaume's eyes. He gave her a smile. She had given him a distraction from his panic, and it was helpful.

A comfortable silence fell between them for several moments.

"I think you should ask the students why they came to the school in the first place. I have my thoughts as to why, but I think they can phrase it much better than I."

Whether that would be a solution or fall flat, Alex wished that the other problems that had arisen would be just as easy to manage. But she was not holding her breath. For now, she focused on her friend and the need to turn things around where he could.

Guillaume knew she would never steer him wrong, and although she could easily compliment him, she had a bit too much on her plate to give undivided attention to him. And he needed to hear it from multiple sources. Frankly, he needed to see why he mattered to all, not just one. In turn, she was certain her friend would collect himself and take back how his school was being perceived. The students would fight for him and the school; of this, she was certain.

After a quick faire la bise, Alex left him to his new mission and to pick out a nice bottle of white wine for his evening meal.

"What is the reason for using room temperature dairy when preparing your baked goods?' Alex asked.

She waited to hear Jones pipe up but was greeted with silence. She turned from the chalkboard. Most of her students were looking out the window, and the students not following her lesson were busy watching the students looking out the window.

"What is more fascinating than creating the perfect blueberry muffins?" Alex asked.

"The cutest black rabbit going mad," Jones supplied without breaking his gaze out the window.

Curious, Alex walked to the window to see a tiny, short-haired black rabbit running a short distance, stop, turn, then run and leap in the air.

"Maybe it got a hold of some jimson weed," Davian offered.

"The rabbit, leporidae, are known for expressing their excitement or joy in different characteristics which include running, spinning in the air, landing, then repeating. The action is known as binking," Jones added. "See?"

On cue, the long-eared black rabbit did it again.

"Doesn't that bunny know that this is the most dangerous place for it to live? It's a cooking school for goodness sakes!" Braxton said.

"Save yourself, petite lapin, before the savory class catches you and eats you up!" Davian added. His voice held a touch of emotion that hinted that he was not joking as his classmates had been.

The black ball of joy stopped as soon as it began then stayed rooted in one spot. Waiting.

Coming into the view of the window was Josephine wearing dark bib overalls, holding a net overheard. Alex put a hand over her mouth to stifle a laugh.

"Looks like rabbit is on tonight's dinner menu," Davian said.

Most of the students gasped in horror at the very mention. If anyone on the savory side saw the exchange on the grounds below, Alex was certain the conversation would be different.

Different in a "drafting up an ingredients list and starting the stove to boil water" kind of different.

Alex sat for a moment, and the visuals of what could be the rabbit's fate lingered in her head. She removed her chef coat and excused herself before leaving the room. Half a dozen pairs of feet followed her, and one set of wheels rumbled.

"I'll be right there," Ren called out as she rolled herself towards the second floor elevator.

Everyone was at the front entrance and on the grounds near the potager's east-facing garden area where the bunny sat nestled in the grass. The moment that the group of students walked towards it, the bunny hopped a foot away. One of the chefs from the savory side appeared opposite from Alex and closest to the bunny. The bunny hopped back towards Alex while Josephine stood with a net.

They all stood at a crossroads of sorts at the whim of a three-pound ball of cuteness. Alex let out an exasperated sigh, turned towards the raised garden bed, removed a few pieces of greenery from the carrots, and walked towards the rabbit.

Josephine gasped in horror, and Alex was certain the Scottish woman was torn between cursing and fainting over the marring of her perfect garden. Alex crouched down and held out the vibrant carrot ends.

The bunny hopped to Alex and began nibbling the greenery.

"I think it's snorting. Is that normal?"

"Binking or snorting is one of the many ways rabbits can show their happiness or excitement," Jones provided.

Alex put out a tentative hand. Her fingertips touched the fur. The rabbit didn't flinch but continued to consume the treat. Once done, it hopped closer to her, waiting. She looked back at the garden to see if she could get another vegetable for it.

"Don't. You. Dare," Josephine hissed. Her face full of

outrage was so out of character for her that Alex let out a little laugh.

Alex kept petting the rabbit. The bunny hopped closer to her pant leg and began munching on it. "No," she giggled.

"Chef Alex has a pet," Braxton said.

"Or a meal," Davian countered.

The rabbit nestled close to her. "I will never make you a meal. What are we to do with you to keep you safe? This cooking school would be vicious for a little thing like you."

Deciding to be bold, Alex scooped a left hand under the rabbit, and the creature didn't fight, flinch, or move. She scooped it up into both hands and cradled it in the crook of her left arm and pet it with the right.

It began snorting like a piglet. Alex LeBeau had just acquired her first pet.

"I don't know if it's a boy or a girl, but what shall we name it?" she asked, stroking its fur.

Ren rolled her chair forward onto the grass. "Petit Déjeuner?"

The class laughed.

Alex looked at the bunny nestling into her arm, licking her hand. "Déjeuner," she whispered, and the ironic name translated in English as *breakfast* fit the black rabbit just fine.

The bunny was only allowed in the classroom for safety in regards to itself and humans. They had no hutch to place the creature in, so each student took turns handling the creature as they studied.

Petit Dejeuner's presence seemed to help Mr. Jones the most as he stroked her fur. Alex spotted the tiny pink tongue darting out to lick his thumb, and Mr. Jones' mouth broke into the first smile Alex had witnessed.

Despite Alex being focused on the history of eggbeaters, her mind was wandering.

"A lazy chef had gotten it into her craw to produce more

with less effort while on a trip across the country by steam train after seeing the train's flywheel combined with a crank providing a continuous rotary motion. She applied that to the hand-turned eggbeater. Some trial and error brought a steam-powered motor into the kitchen to create a standing mixer. For an individual chef or small restaurant, the cost to purchase one was prohibitive, but for Guillaume? Well, his twenty years of networking allowed him to have a new invention that only broke half the time."

Even as Alex helped her students, her mind would drift back to the airship guest list. Even if Guillaume had the list, it would not mean much to them if either of them could not discern if someone was truly a stranger to Brookmeyer.

At the end of class while the students were cleaning up, Alex used that time to fill out lesson plans for the following few weeks.

By the end of the day, word had spread of Chef LeBeau's pet rabbit, and a hutch had been found and delivered to Guillaume's office filled with treats and bedding for the cookery's new mascot.

Amazing how the world kept revolving as if nothing catastrophic were happening in her life and that of others closest to her. Her students knew she was not completely focused, which was dangerous in a kitchen, but today was mainly practice.

Practice.

Alex's hand hovered around the paper she had been jotting down notes on. To construct Rueben's popcorn cannon machine must have required hours of preparation and practice runs to get it right.

Such a machine was not likely ever created before his, which would mean there was a place for Rueben to have practiced prior to the airship dinner that night.

Someone must have seen the machine, whether in sketch

form or physical, in order to re-engineer the popcorn cannon to work as a weapon.

Who would be privy to the work area or could get a hold of a very private item like an engineer's sketchbook?

Alex would have to look into Brookmeyer's schedule during her months with the engineers along with finding out where they formulated a lot of Brookmeyer's blueprints.

They had all been meeting in Honfleur, and Alex had thought it for Brookmeyer's residence, but what if it had been due to hiding the finished product of the blueprints in plain sight?

She had watched the Furious Angel jump out of an airship but was not aware of where she landed. Brookmeyer had been heavy into aviation, but Élie and Rueben had engineering skills, but there was something more. The world had already been in the throes of innovation in terms of airships and flight, but what if they had been onto something completely revolutionary?

Something brilliant enough to kill someone over?

Something had been stolen out of the Damask Hangar, and the police officers could not search for it. How did you search for an item you never saw?

In fact, Alex wondered why the engineers were never questioned or asked to give a sketch of the machine for the officers to find.

Alex thought back on Élie running from the police station the night of the fireworks incident. Élie most likely feigned ignorance, fatigue, or both.

Perhaps he had bought himself time before he could catch back up to the Furious Angel?

. . .

There were too many questions running through her mind, but she kept falling back on the night of the murder on the airship.

Rueben's machine had given the clues, so how come she did not realize it until just this moment?

"Because the popcorn cannon was a distraction," she whispered under her breath.

She closed her eyes and recalled the diorama surrounding the machine. Alex had thought it decorative, but a few things were in spots that should not have been there, including an oil slick.

Not oil but a shaving of gelatine. The same gelatine that photographers use before the change in materials for taking photographs. Had she picked it up, rubbed it between her left forefinger and thumb against the healing nick from a few days prior, would it have stung like lemon juice...like silver nitrate?

Could it be that simple? Could they find Furious Angel by that clue alone?

CHAPTER 20

As soon as class ended for the day, Alex practically ran to the police station.

"I need to speak with Officer Meckelson or Potkiss," Alex said at the front desk as she tried to catch her breath.

"They are off duty."

"What do you mean, off duty? They are always here."

"Ma'am, they hafta sleep sometime."

Alex looked around. "Is there another officer I can speak to that works with either officer?"

"Dunbridal. You can ask for Dunbridal," the officer said with a jerk of her thumb towards the back of the station.

"Merci," Alex said and searched for Officer Dunbridal.

"Ma'am, I brought these chocolate bars for you and your officers to share."

Dunbridal's face perked up, and she reached for the gift offered.

"Officer?"

"Yes, ma'am," Dunbridal said, mouth full of tropical fruit confection and bittersweet chocolate.

"Do you all have any more leads on the person who killed Madam Brookmeyer?"

Dunbridal shook her head. "I mean I am not at liberty to say."

Alex slid into a seat beside the desk and whispered in Dunbridal's ear all that she had concluded and finished with the gelatine.

"I can't say if it will lead to anything, but I'm wondering if it may be the old gelatine used. If so, you can try backtracking where the gelatine plates were sold."

"If they were purchased in town or in state, we may be onto something, but if purchased elsewhere..." Dunbridal shrugged her shoulders then closed her eyes as she devoured the chocolate bar.

"You're right. It could be a bust. If you officers are too busy, I could go investigate it myself."

Dunbridal's eyes bulged. "No. That isn't necessary, ma'am."

"I'll look into it with Officer Meckelson and Potkiss. All right?"

Alex smiled sweetly at Dunbridal, thanked her, and took the remaining two bars with her to the back to greet Pierre.

He was napping, so Alex left a bar for him and promised the last bar to the jailer if she made sure to give one to Pierre when he awoke.

The jailer took her first bite, and from the look on her face, Alex knew that Pierre had a fifty-fifty chance of getting the treat his mother had left him.

On her walk home, she ruminated.

. . .

After a restless night of sleeping poorly, the next morning, bleary-eyed, Alex stood next to a cake platform with a wooden dowel in her grip. Her students stood on the other side of the cake.

"When creating more than one couture cake, you must have stability from some place. This Mad Hatter cake, in this weather, needs well-placed dowels."

Alex rolled chocolate dough on the base cake. "When working with chocolate dough," she continued, "the conditions have to be dry and cool. Meaning no cakes will ever survive the year-round humidity in Honfluer."

The students laughed.

That morning was unusual for the students. There was no lecture or focused demo. They were free to work on something they felt needed more practice in their repertoire before they began their internship at the restaurant.

Alex used that time to tackle inventory in the pantry room away from the demo kitchen. Mundane, but the task brought her an unreasonable amount of joy.

At the far corner of each wing stood a room converted into a pantry. Three of the four walls were lined with black walnut shelves supported by galvanized iron pipe corbels. The lowest shelf was three feet from the floor. An overly long, custom-made dry sink sat along the fourth wall with several rows of turnbuckle bracketed shelves with hooks attached to the shelf underneath to hold freshly picked herbs for drying. It gave a sense that it was floating.

"Damn it!"

Alex popped her head out the entryway and looked at the demo kitchen on the pastry side of the building.

Davian slammed the hot tray down on the table and threw the oven mitts down beside it.

So much for quiet.

In silence, Alex went to Davian, turned him to face towards the doorway, and guided him to the stock pantry. The multiple, aptly labeled metal tins and amber jars made the space look like an apothecary. Alex pulled on the dry sink drawer handle. Three rows of rattan baskets at the base of each drawer held onions, potatoes, or other root vegetables.

She avoided them and walked him toward the back while saying, "You cannot rely on this or any oven for exact temperature measurements. Even if it's calibrated correctly, things happen, and you have your sight to help you. Use that to catch clues. Your cakes are continually coming out dry or unbaked in the center."

Davian's jaw firmed up, and his mouth tightened.

She continued walking him back.

The center of the room was an efficient use of wooden bookcases with two galvanized pipes attached to the tops of each case for stability. Each bookcase back butted up to another back, and the four pairs for pantry cases were parallel to the front entrance. There was plenty of space to move about the center, but Alex guessed that would change as the student attendance grew.

"When you're at the dock, I bet you have one hell of an eye in discerning what is what, yes?"

"Yes," he choked out. "Maybe."

One pantry held various oils for cooking, salts, canned items, vinegars, and other similar items for the savory side. Its twin pantry held canning jars filled with natural colorants, sugar paste, pearl sugar, colored sanding sugar, golden syrup, marzipan, and other items that assisted the dessert making or finishing process of the sweet side.

A smile played at the corner of her mouth. "Pull from that skill; bring it here," she said, gesturing the room to make her point. "You are choosing incorrect flour for your recipes."

His face began to redden.

"When I was in a foreign country, I couldn't read a lick of anything if it was not labeled in English, so I had to go by what I could feel. Come here," she said, grabbed him by the shoulders, and led him to the pantry.

She faced him towards the barrels of different flours and granulated sugars that sat underneath the three walls of shelves.

She opened each top. "Take a pinch with this hand, and grab a pinch of flour from that barrel with the other. You can feel the difference."

Davian nodded.

"Sometimes, when I'm not focused, I'll not slow down and read what's in front of me. I think you may be like me in that regard."

Davian's eyes filled with embarrassment.

"I misread things whenever I'm in too much in a hurry. Sugar and salt is one mistake I made but not anymore even though I did not live it down for years."

Davian looked at her as if waiting for a reprimand.

"What I'm saying is to take a minute before you misread something. If you are unsure, ask. Check and recheck. Okay?"

Looking relieved, Davian nodded.

Alex felt a little bit better about his time at the restaurant. In this interaction, she also had an idea for the next day's lesson.

She stayed after the students had left to sketch it out on paper, but halfway through, her thoughts wandered back to Élie, the blueprints, and Brookmeyer.

With the officers looking into the potential lead on Furious Angel's whereabouts or residence, Élie's were still a mystery.

Perhaps Furious Angel and Élie had been working

together, but how that tied Heston to it all, she could not fathom.

Heston had worked at the Wild Mare, and maybe he had met Furious Angel there? Once again a reach, but she had no other options or leads to go on. Only a hunch.

A hunch that, as the hours passed in the kitchen, Alex was unable to let go. The answer to her query resided in the brothel.

Perhaps one of the workers at the brothel had overheard something between Chef Heston and Furious Angel. Perhaps behind closed doors, they would be more likely to talk with someone other than a police officer. A client.

The more she thought about it, the more it made sense.

Alex thought to ask Eva for her help but knew she had a show later that evening.

Could she convince Josephine to go? The last time they were together, they wound up at the police station. Lighting could not strike twice if they were cautious, she told herself.

Alex worked at the school for a few more hours, hoping to catch the potager before she began her night shift making stocks.

"Good evening."

Alex awoke in a start, unaware of her surroundings for a moment.

Josephine was looking at her.

"Musta fallen asleep waiting for you."

Josephine looked at her through her eyelashes. "Chef Alex was waiting for me?" she asked. The tone in voice made Alex suddenly feel like a school girl.

"You need to go where again?" Josephine slowly asked as they walked away from the school building.

"To the Wild Mare," Alex explained for the second time.

"You do not need me there for moral support. I am happy to stay behind. I mean, shouldn't we maybe have a few outings alone...by ourselves to see if we're a match before we invite another in? Or invite ourselves out? Or however that works?"

Alex rolled her eyes then explained her reason for needing to go to the brothel.

"Oh," the Scot said simply. "Well why didn't you say so?"

"You are all right with pretending to be a couple?"

Josephine gazed at her reflection in the oblong mirror near the front door. "What does it entail? We'd say we're a couple looking to add some spice to our relationship and who would like to be watched as we enjoy each other's pleasure?"

Alex stared and blinked at Josephine's mirrored reflection. Her mind swirled with indefinite scenarios, all involving the charming Scottish woman. "Y-yes," she said weakly, "something like that."

Josephine turned to face Alex. "Sounds like fun. Let's go!" she said and let herself out of the house.

Really need to start thinking my plans through a bit more, she thought, following Josephine out the door.

They were greeted at the entrance by a tall, willowy gentleman who called himself Mr. Drake.

"Miss Miel will be beside the pink and black loveseat," he informed.

Miss Miel caught Alex's gaze and smiled warmly then got up from her seat. She shooed the gentlemen away with a wave of a hand and crossed over to Alex.

"Good evening. I'm a little surprised to see you here, but don't worry. We are discreet for all women and their preference. Speaking of such, which is yours?"

Alex stumbled on her words.

Miss Miel called one of the gentlemen to her and whispered in his ear. A few moments later, not one but three men arrived.

"You can pick all of them if you so choose, or one or two. It depends on what you're in the mood for, my dear."

Alex did not want to imagine what mood she needed to be in for all three men. She needed to get through this without there being much room for error.

"All of them."

Miss Miel smiled at Alex. "Before you begin your festivities, let's discuss the money arrangement," she said and politely guided Alex to a small drawing room. She gave a hard number for each half hour, and Alex gulped.

"No refunds?"

Miss Miel's eyes narrowed.

"I meant in the first five minutes if I don't feel comfortable with either man."

Miss Miel was silent.

The woman knew how to say no loudly without saying a word. Alex gave an inward pout, knowing that she'd soon be parting with her money for a transgression that would never take place.

Alex gave a nod of agreement, and Miss Miel told her the House Rules and Policy. Alex gave the woman her hard-earned money. Alex could not believe she was paying to catch a thief.

After payment, the ladies followed Miss Miel out of the drawing room and up the stairs to a generous room to wait.

When Miss Miel left them, Josephine turned to Alex. "What now?" she hissed.

"Now, we explore other rooms and talk to clients."

"Talk to clients?" Josephine looked horrified.

"Maybe."

The door opened. Three finely dressed men stepped into the room. One was blond, another brunette, and the other a redhead. They were the living embodiment of Neapolitan ice cream.

"Perhaps I spoke in haste," Josephine said. Alex grimaced at her, and Josephine shrugged.

Blonde stepped forward and began pouring some sweet tea while the second walked forward. Red made his way behind Alex and began unbuttoning her blouse from the back. Alex squirmed away.

"Let us not worry about my general state of undress. I prefer to be completely clothed," she lied.

The men seemed to believe it to be a signal, and all three began to undress.

"No, not the shirt!" Josephine told the first one. "And not your tie," she said to the redhead.

"Sirs," Josephine said. "May we speak with you about a Mister Heston?"

Ignoring Josephine's query, the brunette began taking off his trousers.

"There was a regular worker with you that went missing a few weeks ago," Alex prompted.

The men shook their heads. "We only began working here a few days ago," the redhead provided.

Both Alex and Josephine backed away towards the bed, watching the men all in various states of undress.

"How do we get them to stop?" Josephine hissed.

Alex did not stop watching the men standing before them. "I know the answer, and I am certain I am not woman enough to be a part of that kind of solution."

Out of the corner of Alex's eye, Josephine nodded her head in agreement.

"Wait!" both ladies yelled, and all three men stilled.

"I can't do this; I'm not this sort of woman," Alex said, re-buttoning her blouse.

Josephine guided her towards the door. Red tried to reach out to caress her, but she looked down at his trousers at a pool around his ankles and burst into a fit of giggles.

Josephine stopped and looked at him then Alex. "Keep it together."

"I am trying, but I am nervous!"

"We will be right back," Josephine offered before dragging Alex out of the room.

"Where are we going?"

Josephine gave a quick knock on a bedroom door. The loud thwack echoed through the hall. She tested another room. With was no answer, she cautiously cracked open the door then wide, yanked Alex in, and closed the door behind them.

Alex began looking through the dressers and nightstands while Josephine kept on the lookout.

"Someone is coming."

Alex placed everything back how she found it and pulled Josephine into the oversized armoire. The click signaled the firm close of the door. The interior had just enough height that Alex did not need to slouch, but its width was not generous, and she and Josephine were close enough that bosoms touched, and the soft, sweet breath of Josephine played on her cheek. Alex could hear her own heart beating in her ears.

They would exit as soon as the attendant left the room.

"Hurry, Miriam, before they catch us!"

"This room is free. Let us congregate here," a deep male voice rang out, followed by three distinct, high-octave laughs in agreement.

"No," Josephine said. She voiced both their miseries in a single word.

Perhaps the randy group would rather a larger room to party in.

Low whispers, pulling out a drawer then slamming it shut, and a giggle gave her no clue of the choice made.

"Ah. Here it is. A saddle!" the gentleman said with delight.

A thud against the wall followed by breathless kisses answered Alex's internal question as a resounding no.

"Will your friend be joining us tonight?"

"Unfortunately, it appears he has decided to no longer offer his services."

All three women let out a disappointed groan.

"It just means more for you, dear sir!" one of the women exclaimed.

He let out a happy sigh, "Ladies, you do know how to make a man feel welcome."

"Well, it was Miriam's birthday wish to go horseback riding," one of the ladies offered. The rest of the group laughed, then a quiet fell over them as clothed bodies pressed against one another. The drag of billowing skirts being drawn up high enough, Alex guessed, for a well-skilled hand to find its way—

One of the women let out a low moan.

"Let's give the birthday girl a present, shall we?" the gent offered.

Miriam's friends enthusiastically joined in the fawning. Miriam's moans were soft and low as the gent gave words of encouragement, instigating the scene unfolding before them of this erotic birthday celebration.

"Yes, right under hood..." Miriam moaned again. "Dearest Violet, but you do have a skilled mouth."

Alex shifted uncomfortably and slowly in the armoire as to not make noise.

"Before things end before they start, would anyone like a pony ride?" he offered.

"Oh, Violet! Do hand Miriam the riding crop!" a third lady's voice said.

Twack.

"Yaw!" cried Miriam, and the women cooed.

"Just look at how Miriam's posture never wavers," Violet noted, her voice a sudden air of refinery.

"Such command on such a powerful beast!" the third lady said in posh agreement.

Twack!

Alex began to think she needed new friends that offered

such enthusiastic encouragement in the bedroom. One dare call it uplifting, even inspiring.

Twack!

When the gent let out a happy neigh, Josephine almost lost her composure.

Alex slapped her hand over Josephine's mouth to keep her muffled.

The scene went on for several more minutes as each dignified lady took turns riding the saddled man.

"You are such a good horse," the third lady said. "I believe he should have a treat."

"Oh yes. A treat."

Silence, then the sound of slurping. The gent let out a weak whinny.

Alex threw Josephine's hand over her own mouth to muffle her own laughter.

They had to give credit. The Wild Mare gentlemen knew how to give a thorough interactive session that fulfilled the guests' fantasies without question or judgment.

Breathless, the gent offered, "Why don't we take this to the bed?"

A moment of quiet surrounded them. Then the sound of adjusting, removal of more confining clothes and saddle.

Miriam called out. "Joy, come. Come close, and let me see the beauty of your mons. I have longed for you. Please give me this birthday wish."

"Yes," the fellow said, encouraging. "Ladies, you do make a beautiful pair. Do not be shy. We are all here to enjoy one another. I shall wait my turn."

Apparently that was all the encouragement needed. "Oh, dearest Miriam!" followed by a rustling of more clothes being removed, moans rising slow and steady in octaves.

Silence and then Joy let out a delighted gasp. "Oh, Miriam!"

"Ladies if you could see what I see..." The moans continued. Then a breathless male voice, "Violet, may I enter you
from behind?"

"Please, yes," Violet gasped for air. "Please."

The bed began to squeak.

"Harder," Violet breathlessly commanded. "More."

"Violet, don't take your tongue away," Miriam begged.

In the back of her mind, Alex began to question the life
choices that brought her to this very moment of hiding in a
dark armoire with an achingly charming woman and joyful
hedonists on the other side of the dresser.

Alex could feel Josephine's breath on her hand increase
and her own as well. Alex began to rethink her stance on
exhibitionism being unnecessary in adult play. Both ladies'
hands fell from each other's mouths as the moans began to
rise and stagger.

A break of silence in between the moans then both
women let out long moans followed by tension-released
giggles.

"I could use a cigarette," Josephine whispered, making
Alex choke back a laugh until tears rolled down her face.

"And what about you, my dear? You have been left out of
the festivities," the man said and made a clucking sound with
his tongue. "That'll not do."

More rustling of clothes then heavier breathing with the
kissing. Despite herself, Alex leaned towards the armoire
door facing the foursome.

The man cried out. She startled.

"Oh, madam, what a mighty skilled tongue you have!"

The other two women tittered as the slurping sounds
increased. No need to guess what the third woman was doing.

Alex felt a wave of heat in the armoire. When did it grow
to be so hot in this air-conditioned space?

Slurp, slurp. Moan. Soft giggle. Slurp.

Sexual frustration in the guise of irritation fell over Alex as the seduction continued.

"Miriam. Oh. Oh my, Miriam. Yes," the other woman breathlessly said.

Alex desperately tried not to imagine the scene happening only a few feet away from them on the other side of the armoire.

Josephine adjusted her footing inside the armoire. Their breasts brushed against one another, making Alex clench her jaw.

This was by far the worst idea she had ever had, and the more the moaning and knocking of the bed against the wall increased, the more she scolded herself for thinking of it in the first place. She wondered if Josephine was upset with her.

"Josephine," she whispered.

"Y-yes?" she asked. Her low voice was thick, heavy with desire, not anger.

Alex froze. She had not thought of this scenario.

Josephine reached out and touched Alex's hand. The space became too hot, and she was wearing too much clothing.

Worst idea ever.

Josephine's body slowly pressed against her own. The feel of her warm breath fell on Alex's full lips, letting her know just how close Josephine's face had been in the armoire. Very close. Too close. She only had to lean in just a bit, and she and Josephine would have their own party in the armoire.

Just their luck, one or both of them, by a miracle of science, would find themselves with child due nine months to the day after this night.

"Wait," the man called out. "I don't want the party to end so soon. I have an idea. Go into the armoire for one of my games."

Josephine and Alex froze.

Bright lights pierced through the open door and onto Alex and Josephine. Alex wished that the armoire was deep enough to fall into and never return. The women in various states of undress stood still, a frozen look of surprise on their lips as Miriam straddled upon the gentleman's face.

"We didn't order the orgy," Miriam said.

A muffled query came from inside the horse head.

All the women in the room, including Josephine and Alex, turned to the man lying nude on the bed.

The gentleman pulled off the paper mache horse head. "I said, how about a game of Ring Toss? Oh, look. You've brought friends."

Alex did a double take. She recognized that face!

"Mister Karsci!" she said in horror.

No one noticed the bedroom door open.

Élie Karsci's wide eyes held her gaze as he slowly pulled a pillow over his naughty bits.

"What are you doing here?" she shouted.

Indignant, Élie asked, "Ma'am, I would ask the same of you."

"I think," Miss Miel asked from the open door, "we are all wondering the same."

J osephine held her hand as they waited in the police station lobby for the officer to speak with them. Alex had asked if they were in trouble but only received a firm look and a motion to stay seated. The look of annoyance was one she understood due to being on the receiving end more times than she cared to admit.

Josephine squeezed her hand.

Being on the receiving end of, dare she say, a deserved reprimand was humiliating. She could not explain herself out of this situation. Looking for clues and answers and bypassing the officers to do it would not bode well.

She was well over thirty years of age and feared her mother's disappointment.

"Excuse me, officer. May I ring my mother?"

CHAPTER 23

Josephine, Alex, and Élie were led into a room to give their statements to what looked like a long-suffering Officer Potkiss.

"I figured that if you discovered my relationship with Madam Brookmeyer, you would suspect me as killing her," Élie explained.

"Did you? Kill her, I mean?" Potkiss asked.

Despite Élie's disheveled hair and half-tucked-in dress shirt, he managed to look refined even as his face showed his insult at such a query.

"Why ever would I kill the person who kept me from starving?" Élie asked.

Both the officer and Alex's shoulders drooped with that logical explanation.

"But that still does not explain why you were at the Wild Mare," the officer stated.

Alex turned to Élie and saw red creep up his cheeks.

"It was not something I planned. They, the women... Miriam was celebrating her birthday, and I had found myself in need of a shower."

Officer Potkiss held up her hand. "Whoa. Imma need you to start from the beginning of when you escaped the night of the fireworks going off in the station."

"It is not really a story of interest," Élie said.

"I will be the judge of that because so far, this whole case and all the players," Potkiss glanced at Alex. Alex returned her gaze, her mouth in a soft smile. Potkiss continued, "Have made this the most bizarre I've ever seen."

Alex frowned and scrunched up her face.

Did the officer just call her bizarre?

Alex made a note to never give Officer Potkiss another chocolate again. That'd teach her. Alex wanted to stay offended, but Élie's confessions of the missing nights were more important for her to know.

"As I mentioned before, I thought I would be charged for Madam Brookmeyer's murder. Between us being attacked that night, Rueben being kidnapped, and this happening after I gave her the blueprints the night of the dinner party, I was certain you'd charge me."

"But why would you lie about the blueprints? You were forced to give them to Fu—DeWinter, so why lie about it?" Alex asked.

Officer Potkiss cleared her throat. Alex looked over, realizing she had overstepped her boundaries. She gave the officer a weak smile.

"Yes, why did you lie about the blueprints?"

"I thought she would go away and leave Rueben and me alone if I didn't mention anything to the police. She had just killed Madam Brookmeyer," he replied, emphasizing the philanthropist's surname. "If she was willing to kill her, I did not think she would think twice in throwing me, an engineer, off the airship without a parachute."

"The night of Rueben's kidnapping..." Officer Potkiss dropped the query for a moment, letting Alex and Élie anticipate her conclusion. "You invited Mr. LeBeau into your temporary residence despite knowing he was not allowed to speak about or engage in technology discussion."

Élie looked at Alex. "He's a bright boy. Very bright. He came to us," he explained to Alex before turning to the officer. "What was I supposed to do when a young man with that kind of potential visits? Turn him away?"

Élie did not allow the officer to cut in.

"I had planned for us all to have tea, answer some of his queries, then send him home. Rueben and I had been quarreling about what steps to take since our funding was gone. Pierre's arrival was a welcomed break from the disagreement. Rueben wanted me to search for another philanthropist, but..." Élie's words faded. "I didn't want to put anyone else in harm's way. It seems that this project has been cursed, and like I told Rueben, I wanted nothing more to do with it!"

Élie's words rang through the room.

Officer Potkiss was silent for several minutes before speaking. "Mr. Karsci?"

Élie looked up at her.

"Mr. Karsci," she began again. "You were the senior engineer on this project. Why didn't DeWinter kidnap you instead? Clearly, you had more insight into the blueprints and how the machine functions."

Élie sat so still that Alex questioned if he was listening let alone listening.

"I told you. I am not the best of engineers."

Officer Potkiss sifted through papers. "Yes. Yes, I remember you saying that, but what I am missing is how such an average, to paraphrase your explanation, engineer would create something so elaborate. An invention so brilliant that it would catch a philanthropist's eye. If I had been DeWinter, I would have gone after you, not Mr. Ormont, the newest engineer on the project. So why not you, Mr. Karsci?"

Officer Potkiss let her words settle on them, and Élie still did not move besides blink.

The officer broke the silence. "Miss LeBeau, I need you to leave."

Alex looked at the officer.

Officer Potkiss stood to escort Alex out. "I'm afraid I need to charge Mr. Karsci with the murder of not Madam Brookmeyer but of his partner. The originator of the machine."

"No!" Élie said, coming to his senses. "I did not kill Alphonse! He was my friend."

Officer Potkiss and Alex stared at Élie in shock.

"I don't know how, but DeWinter must have known about Alphonse creating the machine."

Both Officer Potkiss and Alex sat back down.

"Who is Alphonse?"

Élie's lips slid into a soft smile as if remembering. "He was my best friend and so bright."

Alex watched the smile fade and a sorrow fall behind his gaze. "The world missed out on such brilliance. The things he could create on paper, his designs... If only we had gotten the funding for it all, he would still be here."

"Tell me more of Alphonse," Officer Potkiss said; her voice lost the accusatory tone.

"We had met several years ago in school. He was more interested in design than finding an employer, so I thought it perfect that we look out for one another. With his last design, I thought for sure we would receive a patent for it. When the patent department of the Committee denied our entry, Alphonse was inconsolable for quite some time until one day, he was not. He told me that he knew where to get the money, and he knew that all the debts accrued would be forgiven."

Élie looked up. "I think I knew it was not so certain, but Alphonse looked happy, and it had been a long time since I saw him like that. When he returned, Alphonse was in a dark place. Darker than I had ever seen him. He told me to leave, and when I did not want to, he forced me out and refused to receive any of my communications."

Élie's eyes began to water.

"I should have been there for him. He should not have died, and he certainly should not have done so believing himself alone."

No one in the room moved or spoke for a while.

"His blueprints were missing. I thought he, at the end of his depressed mood, destroyed them. When Madam Brookmeyer showed at my door asking me about Alphonse's whereabouts, I told her. When her husband had died, she had gone through his things and found Alphonse's blueprints. Alphonse had gone to Madam Brookmeyer's husband to request funding, and he must have said no. Madam said that her late husband had made a tragic mistake, but she wanted to set things right. She offered to help make Alphonse's dream a reality, but we needed someone amazing to help finish what was started."

"And that's how Rueben came to be the creator," Alex finished. Élie nodded.

"I am ashamed for not searching for Rueben. I thought I would make things worse. I have already lost so much, and so I thought it wise to just be forgotten. I cannot live on my own. I have no skills besides being kept, it seems, so in my despair, I had snuck into Miss Miel's Bath House to wash up. No one would notice a man using her steam bath next door. Well, no one except Miriam and her very friendly and well-off friends," he said with a shrug.

With this new information, Alex needed to immediately get a hold of Eva. Alex asked to see Pierre, and with an escort to the jail cell, she met with him.

"It is safer if you stay here," Alex said, squeezing his hand through the jail cell bars. "I made you a little something earlier; did you get it?"

He nodded.

"We are so close. The officers and your aunts are working as hard as they can to find Madam Brookmeyer's killer."

"How safe is it for me if it means losing everything by the time I am let go?"

Alex said nothing because he was right. She could not tell him that she'd rather have him alive and that was all that mattered to her.

"I will not lose you again."

Pierre's cornflower blue eyes looked back at her with irritation.

"I am your mother, and it is my job to keep you safe. I

failed before. I will not make that mistake again. I owe you that much."

He slowly pulled his hand from hers and turned away. "If the police are going to that blonde woman's house, then that means I'm safe."

"There is no guarantee she will not have people coming after you. Look at what happened to me and Josephine at Madam Brookmeyer's house. She was anticipating. She is quite clever."

Pierre silently stared back at her then said, "I am tired. I need to get some rest."

He was angry, but as the mother. she knew she was the closest one to receive the misguided anger. It would do no good to try and logic it out of him. They would have to let his feelings run their course and leave him alone.

Before she could get to the lobby area of the police station, Alex spotted Guardian Reid using one of the officer's empty desks. Octavia stood behind Reid.

When it rained, it poured.

Alex crossed over to her and stood for several moments. Guardian Reid looked up and over her spectacles. The feat itself was impressive.

"I would like to speak with you about my son's situation. He is not what you think he is. I would like to request that you delay sending the necessary paperwork until the killer is found and my son is released."

"Per the agreement, Pierre is only allowed to handle level three technology based on the conditions and terms of his legal filings." Reid shuffled her papers in order then continued. "As you were made aware, Misses LeBeau, any terms are null and void if a Mister Pierre Quennell LeBeau is arrested or convicted of a crime."

Alex stared hard at Reid.

"These are the rules. Your son is not being singled out. If

he had simply done his part, then I would not be forced into this situation."

"My son did nothing wrong. He followed the rules, and besides assisting Madam Brookmeyer, my son was not convicted nor arrested for a crime."

"That may be the case, but as it stands, he has been jailed on suspicion of accomplice to murder."

"He is not an accomplice to murder. He is being protected from a murderer. He is under extremely close police protection until the murderer is caught."

"He should not have touched the contraption in the first place," Reid sniffed. Her face was smug with righteousness.

Alex said nothing. Reid was right. Pierre should not have touched the machine in the first place.

"One infraction can lead to a downward spiral, and we know that a boy of his type is destined to take a nefarious path. I am doing you and him a favor. Frankly, he should never have been allowed to have a license."

Alex stepped close. "He earned it."

"Miss LeBeau, I don't need to guess what strings you pulled. Or what paperwork you forged to state that Pierre is gifted in a manner that does not coincide with young men from his type of breeding. You do him no favors filling his head with lies that he is smart enough to handle machinery like that of Madam Brookmeyer's."

Josephine placed her hand on Alex's shoulder.

"I go by the facts presented, not the wishful thinking of someone's mother," Reid said to Alex then turned to Octavia.

"Miss Laiton, I will impart some words that you would do well to heed. Do not let your career be hampered before it begins by loyalty to family. Facts and following protocol come first. It is for the benefit of our citizens that we adhere to such rules. You cannot bend them to fit your personal needs."

Without another word, Guardian Reid continued to file her papers into her satchel.

"If you make a motion to have Pierre's license revoked, I will have to state your lack of witness to that night in question," Octavia said, stepping forward.

Guardian Reid glanced up. "My dear girl, what do you mean?"

"You were to accompany Pierre during the night of the event, but you never showed. Your unreliability put this young man at risk."

Reid looked at Octavia. "That is not true. You know perfectly well where I was. I was working on a case, and you were there to assist due to the sensitive nature of the young men involved."

Octavia clenched her fist. Alex placed her hand on her sister's shoulder, but she stepped forward.

Alex's stomach dropped. Uh-oh.

CHAPTER 25

"Guardian Reid, you need to practice what you preach."

Guardian Reid's face held the condescending smirk as Octavia continued.

"You have been out to find any infraction in order to remove you from doing your job. You have taken half-finished documents on an ongoing investigation and made a judgment based solely on your own prejudice."

The smirk was beginning to fade.

"You are like a codling moth deep inside an apple."

"Octavia," Alex called to her sister.

Octavia opened her mouth to speak.

Reid's face contorted to show how absurd she believed the analogy, but Alex knew her sister. Octavia was not done.

"If left inside, they become maggots and rot the apple from the inside out."

"Octavia," Alex hissed.

Reid's face burned bright, and her lip trembled with suppressed rage.

"The only way to keep them from causing more damage is

to remove them before they can begin to rot in the first place."

The humor from Reid's face left at being likened to a maggot. Alex guessed no one working for the Committee had ever called Reid a maggot. Well, surely not to her face until tonight.

"How dare you speak to me in such a manner? I can and will report you to your supervisor once I get back to my room."

Octavia crossed her arms. "When you do, perhaps I'll let them know how you have been using your position to blackmail families to keep from getting their licenses revoked."

Reid's eyes darted around.

Alex looked at Octavia with wide eyes.

"There are brains underneath this hat, Miss Reid!"

Josephine gasped.

Alex pulled her sister away. "You are making things worse."

"I'm sick of her using her position to bully people."

Octavia was not wrong. Alex wanted to say all those things too, but it would mean putting Octavia's job in jeopardy, not just Pierre's standing with the licensing board. This kind of information could bar him from any and all technology use. Any promise of a better education would dry up. She had to think, and speaking her mind as Octavia had just done was not the way to do it.

Reid shoved the rest of her papers into her satchel, slung the strap over her shoulder, and quickly walked out of the department.

"What have you done?"

Octavia looked at Alex. "What do you mean what have I done?"

"That little scene did not fix a damn thing. Not only has Pierre lost the one thing to hold onto that would give him a possible good life, but his Aunt Octavia may be out of a job too. I hope it was worth it."

Octavia smiled and clapped her hands. "Oh goodness, it was worth everything. Did you see how her smile dropped when I called her a maggot? That was the best birthday present to myself."

Alex scowled. "Your birthday...our birthday is not until the winter!"

Octavia waved a hand. "Details. You understand what I meant."

Alex took a deep breath, her chest puffing up. Josephine stepped in between the sisters.

"I do believe it is best that we all step away from one another before the regret begins."

Alex stared directly at Octavia over Josephine's shoulder. "It already has."

Octavia threw her delicate fingers towards her clavicle and gasped in offence. "Sister? After all that I've tried to do for you. I was only trying to—"

"Make things worse," Alex spat. "Nothing has been resolved. We are worse off than where we began. How could you be so selfish?"

Alex did not wait for her to reply. "Of course you can be self-absorbed; you have no one of your own, so it's easy to act without consequences. Octavia never sticks around long enough to see the destruction she leaves."

Octavia's hand dropped to her side, her eyes filled with tears.

"I do not know what you were trying to prove by taking on a position with the Committee, but it is clear you need to go back to your life as a botanist. Your ability to add any value to—"

"Enough!" Josephine said. "Alex, that is enough."

Alex swallowed, suddenly realizing what she had just done. Octavia's eyes were wide and full of hurt.

"Oh my goodness. I am so—"

Octavia pushed past her. Alex could hear her sobs as she ran from the station.

Josephine was looking at her. Her unreadable dark eyes made Alex want to crawl into a cabinet and hide.

Guardian Reid's prejudice would be granted. Pierre would lose his license and in turn be overlooked for schools. Octavia had risked her new career for her and was rewarded with being told she was not valued.

Alex had made everything worse.

"Josephine, what have I done?" Josephine collected Alex into her arms. "This is broken beyond repair."

<h1 style="text-align:center">CHAPTER 26</h1>

In the middle of the police station, the Scottish woman just held her. There were no words of judgment or scolding looks. There did not need to be.

A throat cleared, and Josephine gently released Alex. They both turned.

"Her name's Maggie," Officer Meckelson said to Alex.

Alex thought her Furious Angel moniker more appropriate.

"Around a year ago, her brother Alphonse committed suicide. For some reason we do not understand, Maggie blamed Madam Brookmeyer for his death, we think." Meckelson continued, "Chef, you were right in having us speak your detective friend Pepperpot in New Virginia."

It took a moment for the officer's words to set in.

"When we took apart Mister Ormont's machine, we found traces of thallium and brucine along with the bits of gelatine near the machine. When we examined Maggie Tabbis' home, we found it."

"What did she say?" Josephine asked.

"We do not know. She was not at the scene when we

arrived. On the other hand, Officer Potkiss had been but is still unconscious at the hospital. As soon as she comes to, we will ask her. As of right now, we are not aware of Maggie's exact location but have narrowed it down to a few."

"What of Rueben?" Élie asked.

Officer Meckelson looked at Élie, her face not revealing a hint of emotion. "We are not sure, but our strongest conclusion is that he is still in Maggie Tabbis' custody and still alive."

Élie gave a broken smile at the officer.

"What can we do?" Alex asked.

"Just let us do our job. We want to find Mister Ormont too."

Alex did not want to tell the officer that they had been waiting. The only thing to show for it was her young son stuck in a prison cell, losing his future all while expected to sit on his hands while his mother waits for another lead.

Alex needed some fresh air to clear her head. She stepped out of the station.

"Cookie," a familiar voice called from the shadows beside the station.

Alex turned to Eva.

Eva walked to her and grasped her by the wrist. "We have to go."

"Wait. I—what happened to your lip?"

Eva waved it away. "Do not ask questions you do not want the answer to."

Alex looked into her sister's eyes.

"There you are," Josephine called from the door of the police station.

Alex turned and frantically waved Josephine to her, ignoring Eva's exasperated sigh.

Alex turned back to Eva, reading her eyes behind the slight annoyance.

Alex's eyes widened in understanding. "You found him."

Eva stepped back further into the shadows. Alex grabbed Josephine's hand, and Josephine stumbled. The fireworks from the previous evening fell out of her unlatched sporran.

"You are still carrying that thing? Be careful," she warned, picking it up and handing it back to Josephine.

Josephine placed it back into the bag.

"We haven't much time," Eva said.

"Time for what?" Alex asked.

"Stop asking so many questions," Eva replied before looking at Josephine. She straightened. "And who might this be?"

Alex slipped her hand into Josephine's.

Suddenly, Eva was out of the shadows, standing tall and offering her hand to Josephine's to shake.

"I am Eva Merchant, the Ring Mistress of the Wicked Night Carnivale. It is a pleasure to meet you Miss..."

Josephine used her free hand to shake Eva's. "Josephine Campbell."

Eva flashed her a dazzling smile.

Alex bristled.

"Oh, Cookie. Do simmer down with those flashing eyes of yours. Out of the three of us sisters, you are the only daughter of Sappho. Please do keep calm."

Josephine chuckled. Alex gave her a side-eye, and Josephine cleared her throat. Eva winked at Alex.

"Miss Campbell, I had not thought to bring another horse for this excursion."

"I'll find another means of transportation. Where are you headed?"

"She can ride with me," Alex offered.

Eva looked to Josephine then to Alex and smiled.

"Not. A. Word," Alex said.

Eva feigned innocence. "I said nothing. Now you, dear sister, get on the horse."

"Where exactly are we going?" Josephine asked.

"To get Rueben."

Josephine stared at Eva. "I think we should tell the police."

Alex glanced at her. "So do I, but I am afraid that they may make a loud announcement and in turn put Rueben in jeopardy."

Josephine said, "Perhaps let's tell someone we know before we leave, and they can tell the officers after we've gone. This may buy us time to get Rueben."

"Or save our asses if we fail," Eva bluntly stated.

"I'm happy to assist," Octavia spoke from the shadows.

Eva, Josephine, and Alex turned.

"We'd thought you had gone for good," Alex said.

Octavia refused to look at or acknowledge Alex's words. "Eva, how long will it take you to get to him?"

"Thirty minutes and then, assuming all goes as planned, fifteen minutes to get him out."

"I'll need the keys to your auto," Octavia said. She held out her hand but still refused to look at Alex.

Alex placed the key in her sister's hand. It was best not to ask her what the plan was for the vehicle. When everything was done, Alex made a mental note that she would apologize to Octavia. Though for now, Alex hoped she did not have to explain to Pierre at a later time.

Eva looked at her flower-adorned sister, whose face looked like as moody and dark as a spring storm. "Where are you going?"

"To raise holy hell after I pick up Guardian Reid for a joyride. I'll give you a half-hour head start," Octavia replied and left the women to the growing doubt that Octavia's comment was not in jest.

Alex mounted the horse then offered her hand to Josephine. Both women followed behind Eva and rode away from the police station under the cover of darkness.

"Furious Angel worked for the Committee," Alex whispered.

"Come again?" Josephine said.

"In the last year, no mention was made of Alphonse's name on the blueprints—at least in the papers. You heard Élie," Alex said. "No one but Brookmeyer, Rueben, and Élie knew of the machine, and from what I'm guessing, it is not something that can be created in less than a year."

"It must have been small enough to steal and move elsewhere, but the question is how?" Josephine added.

Yes. How, indeed?

Alex was quiet as they continued to ride on the back of the horse.

"The balloon!" Alex and Josephine said in unison.

Eva shushed them.

"We thought they weren't able to get the blueprints, but what if that wasn't what they were after at Brookmeyer's in the first place? What if they had touched down *after* having used the balloon to move the machine or perhaps a part of it? What if Brookmeyer's house was a final stop, not a first stop? One last look around before going on their way?"

Josephine didn't respond.

"The entire town was so focused on the fireworks, and if a hot air balloon was floating around, no one would think much except it was someone looking to watch the fireworks from afar," Alex said, thinking out loud.

Alex could feel Josephine nodding against her back. "Though how to hide that machine in plain sight while moving it?"

They both grew quiet again.

Pondering.

"Eva?" Alex finally said.

"Yes, Cookie," Eva replied without looking back.

"You figured this out, didn't you? You know where the machine is, don't you?"

Eva looked back, gave her sister a dazzling smile, and winked.

A few miles later, Eva guided the galloping horses to a trot and away from the pavement. Their horses stepped onto the soft soil behind the second row of trees that ran parallel to the pavement.

Ahead, a mile and a half of overgrown pathway led to a modest mill with part of the roof missing. The mill was as surrounded by brush as the pathway. Though not well lit, Alex saw a shadow pass by one of the side windows.

She leaned in closed to Eva's ear. "What is this?"

"Crosper's Sugar Mill. Where Rueben is being kept," was all she provided. She put a finger to her lips.

In the cover of growing darkness, Alex saw the familiar hangar she and Eva had explored, but as they rode further, nothing seemed familiar. They were getting closer to standing bodies of water, and the mosquitoes were feasting on her banana-sweetened blood.

"It is missing several parts," Alex heard Rueben saying.

"You said that the last time, and we got them for you. I lost good assistants because of you! You are stalling!" Furious Angel replied.

Alex saw Rueben's ragged face, sunken eyes, and pale skin under the lights as he struggled to speak.

"Will it fly?" Maggie shouted. When he did not answer, she stepped closer to him, shouting the question in his face again, holding her gun to his temple. "Will it fly?!"

Rueben struggled to speak, panic contorting his face.

"Yes, but do not kill me," he pleaded.

Furious Angel sneered at him. "You remind me of Heston,

but unlike you, he refused to cooperate. When I found that he was to be on that airship for the party, he had the nerve to say no to getting me the completed blueprints from the airship. Look what happened to him. Pieces of him are in a bayou like confetti."

"Who is Heston?" Rueben asked, stuttering over his words, attempting to buy time.

"It does not matter. Just know that you are destined for the same end if you continue stalling, but unlike him, I won't throw you in the bayou and let nature have its way."

Despite being several hundred feet away, Alex saw Rueben trembling.

"I will be creative. I will make an example of you and your parts."

"But I did everything you asked me to," Rueben cried.

Nausea rose in Alex.

She turned to both women, "Eva, you get Rueben out of here any way you can. I will take on the blonde."

Josephine grabbed Alex by the arm. "Are you insane? She has a gun!"

Alex placed a hand over Josephine's. "It's all right. I have my own weapon," she replied, pointing with her free hand to her copper whisk on her belt.

Even under the darkness of night with the sliver of light coming from the mill, Josephine's face lost its color. "How is that?"

"Eva is going to need your help. Go!" she said to Josephine before sprinting in the opposite direction of the two ladies.

Alex slipped around the corner and managed to find a partially broken window to work her way through. With one leg inside the mill, Alex was pulling the other into the building when she looked to her right and spotted open hangar doors that she could have easily gone through. The rotorcopter was half in the building, waiting to be piloted.

Furious Angel's fist connected with Alex's jaw. The chef's head snapped sideways. Another fist came towards her, and Alex blocked it with her whisk.

Furious Angel blinked. "One would believe a chef would bring a knife to a fight," she said before withdrawing a sword from her cane.

Alex gave an audible gasp, eyes wide in genuine horror.

"What, and ruin one of my precious blades? On the likes of you? Oh, you are seriously mad."

With her left hand, Alex pulled the balloon whisk separate from the handle and, with a flick of her wrist, revealed a collapsible rungu-shaped weapon. With a thumb, she clicked the small switch on the inner handle to electrically charge the signature knob at the end of the melee weapon. The bulbous tip cracked and sparked.

Her opponent cocked an eyebrow, impressed.

Alex tossed the balloon whisk to the side and charged at Furious Angel.

Fencing had never been her forte, and Alex's only goal was to not get perforated. She sidestepped the blonde's lunge, turned quick on her heel, and rapped her on the back. Alex then angled her weapon so the knob touched Maggie's back. The blonde spasmed, her body holding her position as the electricity coursed through her body.

Alex kicked Maggie's side, and she stumbled away but righted herself.

Anything around Alex could be a weapon. Her legs, her free hand, Alex even used her own hair to pull Maggie's bladed hand away. A few cut braids fell to the ground.

Out of breath and panting, she blocked the knife. Furious Angel sucker punched Alex with her free hand. Alex's head hit the concrete, not enough to knock her out but enough to put her in a daze. Alex waited for the next blow she could not move away from, but nothing ever happened.

Furious Angel jumped off of Alex and ran to the steam-powered, counter-rotating rotor aircraft and got inside. Though protected partially in the darkness, the blonde began working the controls. The blades started their rotation, and the cumbersome craft began to lift away from the ground outside the orange-peel-type hangar doors.

Alex rolled to her side, attempting to get up. The blonde was desperate to escape. A firm hand caught Alex's shoulder.

"She's getting away," Alex exclaimed to Rueben.

Rueben shook his head and pointed to Élie standing only a few feet across from them, holding Josephine's sporran. In the other hand was the sky rocket with the India Square Bomb firework attached to it. Élie dropped the leather bag then dropped the firework into a tube. He used the Döbereiner's lamp sitting on the worktable to light it before aiming it towards the machine Furious Angel had just gotten in.

The machine hovered then gained momentum to take off and away from the hangar.

Several long moments passed before the rocket made a loud fwoop sound and discharged from the tube directly towards Furious Angel.

Nothing happened. Perhaps it had gone out before impact, Alex thought.

In answer, the firework exploded inside the control area, consuming Furious Angel and sending the machine crashing to the ground. The blades hitting the ground crumpled upon impact, and the heat from the explosion blasted her in the face. She struggled to stand.

Rueben stood beside Élie, his arm around his shoulder, and they watched their creation burn. Élie's cheeks were stained with tears, and his eyes were filled with a rage and satisfaction Alex had never witnessed before. Rueben stood beside him, watching as their functioning invention went up in flames.

CHAPTER 27

Only moments later, most of the police officers from Honfleur arrived, but neither Guardian Reid nor Octavia were alongside.

The Honfleur volunteer medics addressed Rueben's cuts and gave him liquids and food. Despite the evening temperature being hot as blazes, Rueben had a quilt draped over his shoulders.

"Will he be all right?" Alex asked.

"Yes," Élie said. "I will take care of him."

Alex looked at him and knew he was telling the truth.

"I still don't understand why she kidnapped Rueben and killed Madam Brookmeyer," Josephine said.

"I think I do," Alex supplied. "Though it is a bit more involved than even I expected."

Eva placed a hand on Alex's shoulder. "We should get you to the police station so you can get Pierre. Shall we take the horses back?" she offered to her sister and Josephine.

"Only if the officers do not need us for anything here," Alex said, concern in her voice.

Alex checked in on Élie and Rueben. Both men were

being cared for by the medics and told Alex they would be dropped off at the police station to finish any questioning.

Alex nodded and followed Josephine to one of the horses.

"Momma, I can't breathe," Pierre squeaked out, but Alex did not let go.

"Cookie, hold him while sitting over here. I have a show in three days."

In the lobby area, Alex and Pierre sat down next to Josephine; Octavia sat next to Eva. Octavia still refused to speak to Alex, but Alex surmised that her sister had not taken Reid out for a joyride as threatened earlier.

Once Rueben and Élie were cleared by the medic, an officer requested the two engineers give their statements.

Once they finished, both of them sat opposite of everyone else.

"I feel I owe you an explanation," Élie said in Alex's direction. "I began working with Alphonse in seventy-three. We had drafted blueprints and began creating a machine that would allow us to get to remote areas and disperse medicine through pontoons to those in need. Three years later, our collaboration led to an attempt to patent the rotorcopter through the Committee. After several months of silence from the Department of Patents, they rejected our proposal, and that was all."

Rueben looked at Élie as if with new eyes: eyes of pity and betrayal.

"Last Autumn, Alphonse went to Mr. Brookmeyer in search for backing this altruistic project. Alphonse never knew his mentor's wife, Madam Brookmeyer, had overheard about the plans."

Tears began to stream down Élie's face.

"Alphonse had struggled with so much, and I think," he

stopped, catching his breath. "I think the rejections and other factors came to a head. He had put so much onto Brookmeyer and needed his validation. Brookmeyer did not see the possibility of the machine. It was not personal. Brookmeyer thought highly of Alphonse, but..."

The words caught in Élie's throat. Rueben placed a hand on Élie's shoulder.

Élie found his voice again. "I thought I was his family. He never spoke of having a sibling. Whatever the reason for not mentioning her was probably what made him so set on getting the backing needed from elsewhere. Finishing the prototype and making a full-size rotorcopter was the only thing that mattered to him. Those pontoons on the sides were to hold medicine, carry it to those in need."

Élie stopped, gathering his thoughts.

"The rejection was too much, and he took his own life. I kept...I kept the blueprints because it was all I had left of him. By twist of macabre fate, Brookmeyer died a few months later. I sent my condolences. I did not know Madam Brookmeyer had been looking for Alphonse."

Rueben looked at Élie with wide eyes.

"We, Madam Brookmeyer and I, thought it best never to tell you," Élie said.

"You let me believe it was you, Élie, that had created the rotorcopter," Rueben said, his voice laced with disappointment.

Élie was silent for a few moments, spent.

"Somewhere between seventy-six and late last year was when Maggie Tabbis," Eva said, looking at Alex, "Furious Angel had been sent to work for the Committee, but that was not the path she wanted to stay on."

Alex looked at Eva, noting a new hollowness behind Eva's eyes.

"My...sources found that Furious Angel decided she was

destined to be something greater, which included overtaking the national leader to become a dictator."

"How utterly crazy," Rueben spat.

"I have it on good authority on how the inner functions of the Committee work. They have a department that regulates the amount of new technology that is created in the United States."

Eva stopped to look her audience in the eyes, "Well, Furious Angel lost her brother, the last member of her family alive, and in her eyes, it was the Committee's fault. Her friends didn't know she was suffering. Hell, they didn't know she had a brother. If they had, they would have done anything in their power to keep her from getting this far in her plan," Eva said.

"What plan?" Élie asked.

"To kill off the Committee so quickly that in the devastation and loss, there wouldn't be enough time to elect new Committee members. It would be, in her mind, a way for her to take control. I think she believed her friends would have come around to her view."

Alex stared back into Eva's eyes. It wasn't hollowness in Eva's eyes; it was guilt.

"The pontoons that were originally intended to hold medicine would instead hold poisonous gas that would seep into the drinking water. Or rain over the Committee's headquarters off the Gulf of Mexico."

Everyone's eyes widened, comprehending just how unhinged the woman had grown.

Eva raised her hands, palms out.

The space was silent except for the sniffling of Élie as he tried to hold back tears.

Officer Meckelson had joined the group and was intently listening.

"What I was able to piece together is that after

Alphonse's death, Maggie Tabbis arrived to find that there were no signs of the blueprints anywhere. I am guessing she took what scraps of blueprints Alphonse had lying about in an attempt to 'Frankenstein's monster' the rotorcopter. When she could not finish, she decided to go to Reuben for help because she figured out the reason he was brought in."

They all were still for some time until Élie glanced at Rueben, giving his silent permission to continue.

"When she found out that we were working with Madam Brookmeyer, someone she partially blamed for Alphonse's death, she decided to get rid of the distraction. That way she could have Rueben to herself and be rid of another enemy."

"The rotorcopter never would have taken off further than several feet. I think that is why Mr. Brookmeyer initially refused funding," Rueben quietly added.

With nothing more for Eva, Rueben, or Élie to share, Officer Meckelson informed each of them of the need to complete paperwork before discharging them.

CHAPTER 28

Early the next morning, Alex left Pierre asleep in the quiet house to take a walk along the shore. Her head was spinning with all the adventure the week had brought and the events that still had yet to happen later that day.

Alex was certain her sister was out of a job due to Reid's word and scathing paperwork report alone. Alex was aware that ripping into her sister was uncalled for, especially because Octavia had been correct.

Alex had wanted to say all the things Octavia had said, though probably wouldn't have managed such a scientifically insulting manner. Octavia had many skills, and creative insults were one of them.

But at the heart of the mess was who had brought them to this mess in the first place.

Maggie Tabbis.

Alex had come close to losing Pierre, but it never came to fruition. Not like it had for Maggie Tabbis.

The night before, though only mere hours prior, officers had driven everyone back to their respective homes, but Alex had stayed back as Maman Eloisa and Pierre were escorted back home.

Eva had stayed behind in the shadows, and they talked.

"I don't understand why she would go through so much trouble to kill the Committee. It is simply mad."

Eva just looked at her and simply said, "She lost someone she loved. Grief and loneliness make us do crazy things."

Alex sat with that truth.

"How could anyone bring themselves to take another person's life? To kill? To harm?"

"Oh, Cookie. How I do love that heart of yours. Always a mother, even before Pierre came into our lives."

Alex did not know how to respond to Eva, so she kept silent.

"Anyone is capable of horrific things. I do not care what the Committee says; it does not matter if Anglo or not."

Eva turned to Alex, a quarter of her face shadowed, but the glint of her eyes and stain of her lips captured the light. Eva grabbed her by the shoulders.

"The difference between you and Maggie Tabbis was the life you built. It was the friends you made. Remember that. If you need us, we are here, and you are never a burden."

"I know that, sister."

Eva stared at her for a long time. Alex saw something behind her eyes.

"Eva? Do you know you have us, your family?"

Eva did not speak, but the air shifted.

In that moment, Alex understood. Something was troubling her beautiful sister. Eva the brave. Eva the wise. Eva the utterly infallible.

Alex hugged her sister as tight as she could. "She kept her life a secret from you, all of you."

Eva stood there, unmoving.

"Maggie was an agent, your agent. You sent her to work for the

Committee to gather secrets. You could not have known. It is not your fault."

Alex did not let go, but after what felt like forever, when she thought she should let go, Eva finally returned her embrace.

"Your father used to come out here at all sorts of times of the night to think."

Maman Eloisa's words brought Alex out of her reverie of the night before.

"I did not expect to see you up so early."

"I could say the same about you," her mother replied as she walked to her.

Maman Eloisa slipped her hand into her Alex's and gave it a gentle squeeze.

"Think about what?" Alex asked, following alongside her mother.

Maman Eloisa's face softened, her eyes seeing beyond what was in front of her.

Remembering.

"Not a clue, but each time he came home, he'd smell of the water and have grand ideas for something new to invent."

Alex stole a glance at her mother. A smile played at the corner of Maman Eloisa's mouth. The sort of smile someone has when they are leaving out the part of the story that would be deemed inappropriate or too salacious to speak on.

Alex grimaced at the rise in conflicting sentimental paternal memories.

The whole town knew how Alex's father met his demise. Everyone in town agreed that losing the love of your life was horrible, but all agreed that doing so while in the throes of passion with their spouse was ideal.

Well, ideal for everyone except the surviving spouse.

"And don't you feel bad for not coming home until now," Maman Eloisa said.

"I didn't, I mean..."

Alex didn't look at her mother. Despite her mother's sincere words of reassurance, shame fell over her. They walked in silence for a long time.

Alex struggled to find the words of apologies owed to her mother.

"We know you had your own demons to fight."

They were silent for several minutes.

"I let myself be fooled, and I was so ashamed." Admitting her stupidity out loud hurt.

"I wish you would've come home sooner so I could have helped you."

"I was too embarrassed."

Maman Eloisa nodded in understanding. "Yes, I felt the same after your father's passing."

Alex vaguely remembered the stares because she was too caught up in her grief to comprehend the whispers.

"If it is of any comfort, most of the town still don't know what happened except the truth: Pierre's father died. Those that do know the details are your closest friends and they haven't said a word," Maman Eloisa said and patted her hand.

Alex and Maman Eloisa continued walking then turned around to head back towards the house.

"Maman?" Alex finally said.

"Yes."

"Do you think you'll ever find someone to love again?"

Maman Eloisa chuckled. "I already have."

Alex stopped, stunned, and looked at her mother.

"Oh, you mean a permanent dent in my bed?" Maman Eloisa asked.

Maman Eloisa stopped laughing to take a moment to consider the question.

"Maybe," she replied then turned to Alex. "What of you? Do you think you're ready now?"

Alex thought of lying, but in the past, that resulted in her not coming home when needed the most.

"Maybe," she admitted, "but this time, I am really afraid."

Maman Eloisa leaned up and kissed Alex's cheek. "Me too."

Alex looked down into her mother's face. It took everything in her to keep from sobbing on her maman's shoulder, so she just went back to walking towards the house.

CHAPTER 29

Later that morning, Davian left his gift on the cutting board before walking to the pantry.

He stayed in the space when the wheels on her chair creaked under the entryway board to the demo kitchen. He was forced to watch from the confines of the pantry.

Would she know it was from him?

Would she know how to use the contraption, a magnet spider that could pick up small items she dropped?

Davian had made it from old umbrella and clockwork parts. He put magnets at the feet of the metal arachnid, so it picked up lost metal objects like a chef's knife. The only poor planning was if Ren lost anything in the kitchen near the cast-iron stove. Davian remembered back when he lost two spiders before he solved that problem.

As far away as he was from the table, he could hear the spider's ticking life as it rested on it. Davian was convinced it was a half a second slow.

His plans for leaving it somewhere in the classroom upstairs had been thwarted, but he was grateful for not leaving personal notes on the spider reach and lap desk besides her name.

Ren looked around over her left shoulder and then the right. Davian held his breath as Ren examined the gifts on the table. Her face unreadable, her lips set in a thin line and brows furrowed.

Surely she hated it.

Ren tested the spider reach in the air and then on the floor and smiled.

Davian blinked, and the daydream was gone. Ren was in the room, but no gift waited for her on the table and no note for making amends. He watched her search under a table for something she must have dropped while in class. Empty-handed, Ren wheeled herself out of the room.

Davian curled his hand around the spider he had made for her, un-received.

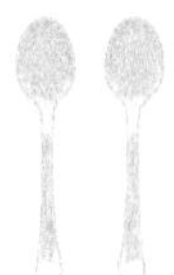

CHAPTER 30

A little after luncheon, the humidity was close to one hundred percent, and Alex knew she would melt. Though as if by some way of magic, the Ring Mistress and proprietor of the Wicked Night Carnivale looked as cool as the deceptively blue sky above them.

Alex kissed her perfectly coiffed sister on the cheek while Eva firmly placed a handled basket into Alex's hand. Alex did not need to guess what was in the cloth-covered basket.

Maple Pecan popcorn, an Absinthe lollipop, Black Cherry licorice squares, and test tube beakers filled with the flavored sugars Alex nicknamed pixie dust.

Alex knew because she had created the menu for Wicked Night Carnivale's soon-to-be stationary performance tent somewhere out West.

Eva pulled away and looked Alex in the eyes, giving her a reassuring smile. Both knew it would be a long while before they saw one another again, and the reason would likely be the same: —trouble.

Alex brushed a falling tear from Eva's soft-rouged cheek. Eva winked, took a deep breath, and collected herself.

"You're going to miss your train," Maman Eloisa said, but all knew it wouldn't leave without her. It *was* her train after all.

Eva kissed the crown of their mother's head, turned, and boarded.

A lex walked Maman Eloisa and Pierre back home, and there, standing at the foot of the steps, was the youngest of the triplets.

Maman Eloisa kissed Octavia's cheek and embraced her tightly before leaving Alex and Octavia behind. Too many goodbyes in one day was too much for her maman.

Both siblings stood in silence.

"I will not be coming back for some time. I did not want to worry you and Eva, but I had been asked to keep a watchful eye on Reid. That is why I was here. Pierre being in the midst of things just happened to be a coincidence and not part of the equation. After what I've gathered on Reid previously, you and Pierre won't have to worry about his license anymore. A lot of her charges won't now."

Alex was at a loss of what to say.

Octavia began to back away to leave. "I need to sort things out," Octavia sniffed.

Always the attention seeker.

Her sister wasn't a bad person, Alex reminded herself. Her sister just made questionable choices sometimes.

"I am sorry for my harsh words yesterday. It was unnecessary. Thank you for putting yourself on the line to help us, your family," Alex stated.

Octavia blinked in surprise. Whatever speech her botanist sister had planned seemed forgotten.

"I made you something," Alex continued. Then reached

into a small, metal tin she had been carrying in her satchel hooked to her belt.

Alex began sifting through, looked at her sister's plumage-filled hat then back at the tin's contents. "Perfect. May I?"

Tentatively, Octavia handed Alex her hat. Alex took out the item and handed her sister the tin to hold.

With a small set of pliers, Alex gently poked the wire attached to the green gum paste orchid stem through the band. After finagling, and satisfied that the sugar flower would stay in place without damaging her sister's head, Alex handed her the hat back.

"So you'll always have me with you...wherever you decide to go."

Octavia looked down at the flower and then back at Alex. For the first time in a very long time, Octavia did not have the last word.

Alex went back to the school to gather the gifts she had made for the first student night at the restaurant. She grabbed the tin filled with the treats out of the staff room before leaving the building, passing the garden.

"Hometown chef makes good, eh?"

Alex tilted her chin down and looked up at the approaching Josephine through her lashes. "Not in the least."

"You know you're in the newspaper? Front page."

"No," Alex said in horror.

Josephine nodded, walking closer to her. "Looks like I know someone famous."

"I am hardly internationally known. Locally known? Yes. Nationally? Not yet."

Josephine stood mere inches from her, looking her in the eyes. "So, locally famous chef, will you leave this parish to seek your fame and fortune?"

"What is out there that I do not have here?" Alex asked. Her face held all the seriousness her heart held.

Josephine did not answer but slipped her hand into hers.

"I would like to call on you, Miss LeBeau, if you give your permission."

"Alex. We've already gone out before."

"No. An outing to a brothel does not count as a proper courting. Well, not for me with you."

Alex's cheeks grew warm. She wasn't embarrassed. Another feeling that was old yet familiar rose within. She could only make her head nod at the beautiful Scottish woman standing in front of her.

Josephine stood reading Alex's eyes.

Alex leaned forward and pressed her lips to Josephine's. With one hand, Josephine drew Alex to her, their bodies pressed against one another. Alex felt Josephine's other hand cradle her nape, and Alex could do nothing but fall into her kiss.

A kiss laced with joy and the promise of mischief to come, and Alex welcomed it all.

They kissed until Alex found herself breathless, and Josephine promised to control herself.

"Not too much, I hope," Alex said, making Josephine laugh.

"Oh, my Alex. You are cheeky," Josephine said with a laugh before kissing her again.

Josephine's lips parted, and her tongue tasted of sweet fruit.

Later in the mid-afternoon, Alex carried the taste of Josephine's kisses on her lips as she walked to the *Cuisine du Monde*, the cookery's student-run restaurant in the heart of town.

There were so many cuisines for the students to

remember because their school's restaurant was known for bringing exotic cuisine to the little port town.

Alex's students were excited despite being given the lowliest jobs in the kitchen.

Traditionally, the pastry class worked on pre-making items for the restaurant during the day so there was no need for an entire pâtissier staff at the *Cuisine du Monde*. The butcher had, with the help of the student class in the morning, already prepared all cuts of meat for the restaurant menu based on what the chef had planned a month in advance. All based on if the crops were good or if prices on the heads of cattle were reasonable.

Her students would get to see how kitchens were managed by numbers more than the muse while engaging in menial work.

Due to the fiery crash and putting the pieces together, not only did the Honfleur police get recognition for solving the case but the cookery also received mention in the local and national papers.

In the coming weeks, Guillaume would milk the media and make sure to sell out reservations each night, making sure the school would stand and be filled with new, talented students for the Autumn semester.

While Alex was joyful over Pierre being freed and no longer under Guardian Reid's eye—or even Octavia's—she wondered who would take the place of a person such as Madam Brook-meyer. Kind philanthropy willing to give men a chance in science and engineering? Not a common trait in the rich.

She would miss what collaboration that could have been and was certain Guillaume would too in terms of the capital needed to run the school. They would just have to figure out a way to get his school noticed, minus the murder and kidnapping.

Alex looked at the students, her students. By society's standards, they were the ones not to bet on.

The young woman in a wheelchair. The fellow meticulous in knowledge but lacking social skills. The older white man starting over in a female-dominated field. And a young white man with a chip on his shoulder but with enough skill to set the culinary world aflame.

Society wasn't always right about things, including the value of people no matter their differences.

Watching her students' enthusiasm over the kitchen duty on their shoulders reminded Alex of when she had been a fledgling chef. She would have never thought she'd survive half the adventures she experienced, but here she was, passing on her knowledge of gastronomy to willing students.

They were good students despite their flaws.

One thing they all had in common was food. They would find their place in the world because of it. They would figure out where each of them fit in their classmates' world because of that one thread that tied them together.

But a few hours before the dinner rush began, the Family Meal was priority and already on the large prep kitchen table.

Second and Senior students sat on the benches beside each other with Guillaume at the head of one table and Chef York at the other.

"You made it!" Guillaume cried when Alex entered the room. "Sit. Sit."

The students made room for her and handed her a plate.

"Mr. G was finishing his story," Davian informed her.

Guillaume waved her to sit beside him. "They searched LeBeau's auto and her trunks and find my couteaux. No, wait. Ellec, what is the word?"

"Knives," she provided.

Alex cut in. "They said I—" she mimicked lifting her skirts, "indecently exposed myself and had weapons. One officer looks at me and says nothing. The other officer, Potkiss, picks up Pierre in her vehicle and drives him to the station. Hours later, Guillaume, desolé. Mr. G shows."

"And why is that, mon ami?" Mr. G asked playfully. Alex did not answer. "Because there is never a time you do not have a run-in with the police at least once in each town you visit."

"Remember Budapest?" she offered.

They both chuckled, and everyone at the table leaned in, hoping for an explanation.

Mr. G chortled. "You were looking after that monkey for that friend of yours, and the coppers pulled us in." Mr. G let out a deep laugh, and it took several minutes before he could find his voice again to say, "There is nothing more difficult than keeping a straight face when trying to answer a copper's questions when your pet monkey won't stop—"

He made a lewd gesture towards his crotch.

The students howled in laughter around the long, wooden table. The stories continued longer than the summer sun stayed in the sky that day.

As the dinner rush began, Alex knew she was finally home.

AUTHOR'S NOTE

Thank you for reading our story. Your purchase of this book could help save a life, offer comfort and support to so many in need.

A percentage of the profits from sales of this story go to American Foundation for Suicide Prevention (AFSP). AFSP raises awareness, funds scientific research, and provides resources and aid to those affected by suicide.

Afsp.org

#StopSuicide

If you are in crisis, please call the **National Suicide Prevention Lifeline** at **1-800-273-TALK (8255)** or contact the **Crisis Text Line** by texting TALK to **741-741**.

ABOUT THE AUTHOR

Nikki Woolfolk (They/Them) is a latchkey kid of film noir, cozy mysteries, and gritty detective novels. Author and Professional Chocolatier, Nikki writes humorous speculative fiction and mysteries with a bite.

www.NikkiWoolfolk.com

facebook.com/NikkiWoolfolkAuthor
twitter.com/NikkiWoolfolk
instagram.com/NikkiWoolfolk
goodreads.com/Nikki_Woolfolk
bookbub.com/authors/nikki-woolfolk

The right chocolate can change your world! Belle Monde Chocolates crafts and delivers high-end confections, making these luxury flavors of chocolates and candies both affordable and accessible.

Calling all Steampunks, Armchair Sleuths, and World-Travelers! Sign up to receive our monthly emails of our *BOOKS &* *CHOCOLATE* newsletter at www.NikkiWoolfolk.com or

www.BelleMondeChocolates.com